ROUT

Saturday 22nd August 1485

Simon Cooper

Penwood Publishing

*To My Mum, My Wife, My Children and
Grandchildren*

*To All those who laughed and mocked and for those
who fail to see past the ends of thier noses.*

to My Brothers.

FORWARD

In 1485 the future of England changed on one day, that day was August 22nd, a Saturday, a bloody morning of hard, hot, sweated, death and dying, many 1000's of men's lives ended in a melay of blood, pain and filth and gore.

A battle of immense proportions, yet in just a few short hours on that hot, damp, and misty morning, the two sides of the wars of the roses met head on in a battlefield nearby to Market Bosworth and history was changed forever.

This is a story, a tale, an imagination involving two brothers, one a blacksmith and the other a fletcher. They live local to the battlefield; they, by being over inquisitive get caught up in the evolution of the battle story.

The story starts a few days before the battle, the troubles bought by an unknown disease also make their mark.

FOREWORD

Lorem ipsum dolor sit amet, consectetur adipiscing elit, sed do eiusmod tempor incididunt ut labore et dolore magna aliqua. Ut enim ad minim veniam, quis nostrud exercitation ullamco laboris.

PREFACE

This is a story, an Imagination, a tale of two brothers, one a blacksmith and one a fletcher, they live close the battle grounds of the Battle of Bosworth Field in the time of 1485.

Being inquisitive and foolish they go to the place of the battle and witness death and gore and the horrors of
battle fighting.

On this day 22nd of August 1485, the future of England changed forever, the formal end of the War of the Roses was concluded and King Henry VII came to the throne.

The death of Richard III was grusome and sudden but witnessed by few. or was it?

"The y'rkists men in tha days of beff're
Square fought hand to hand in a
stench of blud and gore.
All believ'rs did trust in justice are endorsed.
They'd hath followed that King there
just of faith, a wage and because.

Rememb'r well men who is't to tha Anne
Beame on a hill, hath passed this way.
Souls of well men alive beff're the misty
blued dawn on the Augustine 22nd daye,
'Gainst Henry's odds those gents
wouldst not lay down nor yield.
The hath lost souls of men who is't death did
come on the run from redemo'r feld".

ROUT

"b'ffor'tha'words"

In 1485 the future of England changed on one day, that day was August 22nd, a Saturday, a bloody morning of hard, hot, sweated, death and dying, many 1000's of men's lives ended in a melay of blood, pain and filthy gore.

A battle of immense proportions and yet in just a few short hours on that hot, damp, and misty morning, the two sides of the wars of the roses met head on, on the battlefield nearby to Market Bosworth and history was changed forever.

Perhaps, the battle has many names, but the Battle of Bosworth is the most well-known of those names in these parts, the "Battle of Bosworth Fields" is where most will read of its enormous political and reverential impact on the future of an Englishman's life and the development of a new dynasty of the Tudors.

Within the next 100 years; England experienced the formation of the Church of England and the end of the domination in England of the Catholic Church, this may have been a signal of the end of what was understood to be the Middle Ages, or perhaps the dark ages. It is however clear that without the battle and its conclusion, we would not have experienced Henry the eighth, Henry the seventh's son and his colourful life.

This is a story book, it is not so much a story about the Battle of Bosworth Field, although there is a narration as reference to the morning of the 22nd ^{of} August 1485.

This is a story, a tale, an imagination involving two brothers, one a blacksmith and the other a fletcher. They live local to the battlefield; they, by being over inquisitive get caught up in the evolution of the battle story.

In their day the battle took place nearby to a place known as Redemoor, it is a marketplace named as we know it today as Bosworth. (Market Bosworth). They may have seen the King the day before they battle, they may have seen him die a gruesome death on the day of the battle.

Some of the names and places have changed and are in this story as a reference to the historic recollections and the reports on the battles, most of which were written in authority some 30 to 50 years after the battle. So, who knows the real story?

Some say there were more men slain in the "Rout" of the Battle of Bosworth Fields than in the battle itself.

Today's visitors centre for the Battlefield is at a place called Ambion Hill, which overlooks the original place of the battle on the vales leading down to the Fenn Laynes and the boggy marshland that was in 1485.

Ambion Hill is referred to in this book as Ann Beame Hill. There is a name of a place called Sandyfford this is a place which is thought does not exist in name today, although some not so local historians claim they know where it is. In this story these as other place names are somewhere wrapped up in the imagination and a few maybes.

The two characters Jervis and Thomas know where these places are, as they have lived in the area in the 1400's for most of their adult life. They live in a quiet backwater to Market Bosworth called Carltonstone, today it is known as Carlton.

Its whereabouts lays about a mile and a click from Market Bosworth. In 1485 it would have been almost less than a hamlet, it did have a wooden built chapel, it did have several wells, a manor house, and lands where crops were grown, beans and roots. The woods close by were good hunting grounds, as was the fishing in the rivers and streams crossing this part of the county.

Carltonstone was well known for its high quality of crafters and the smithing, leather workers and cap makers made a steady living.

The local market at Redemoor was a good place to sell well made leather goods and household items brought to the market by the likes of the Blacksmith and his brother the fletcher and wood turner.

Our story starts a few days before the battle, the troubles bought by an unknown disease make their mark within the families, in 1483 to 1509 the disease known as the "Swett" or the "French Swett" decimated communities with little or no warning.

Death from the swett occurred within hours, described as:

"a rapid death from the stench of foul vapours around the heart"

It was probably a Hantavirus bought over with French mercenaries, the effect of this epidemic was far reaching economically within the wool farming communities in England and had infected by 1503 most of mainland Europe.

"A rout is the description of a panicked, undisciplined and disorderly retreat of fighting men and troops from a battlefield, following a collapse in a given fighting group of command and authority, of the army's cohesion and combat morale. The word originates from Middle French's "route" a defeat, disorderly retreat,"

Derived from old English and old French and Latin references to "romper" "to defeat", put to flight,", "to break up, smash," going back to Latin "rumpere" and "rumpus".

"RUN"

"Rout"

"Run broth'r, Thomas, scarp'r and
flee f'r thy own life, alloweth us not
beest slain this m'rning, those evil
ffrench's soldi'rs wasteth thy blood,
hold thy belief, tis that we art not
f'r his square, we remain innocent
only of being but a witness to the
death of the sire bogged in the
marshes on Redemoor this day".

CHAPTER 1

"God f'rbid I shall yield one step
from h're at th's battelfeld,
I shall greeteth mine own death with
the lord and as yor king

'r cutteth tha' bastard Tudor down".

Saturday, August 22nd, 1485, England

So, history was written
and legends false and foul were born,
birthed out of blud and treachery
on a red-tinged August morn.

The King Richard III would grant property and land to those Lords who would provide him with soldiers to fight for so many days in a year. They also had to swear an oath of loyalty to the King, and they became his vassals. The Lords in turn granted land to knights the fighting knights. In return, they had to pledge to fight or be available to fight for so many days a year.

However, If a knight had to fight, 50 days a year when those 50 days were up, he would return home even if the King was in the middle of a square (battle).

"Payeth tha 'shield wage'. Those gents hath
used the wage to payeth soldi'rs at which
hour those gents did need those folk".

At the bottom of society were peasants. Most were serfs or villains. They were not free and could not leave their land without the lord's permission, as well as working on their own land they had to work on the lord's land for several days a week.

They also had to work extra days for him at busy times like harvest time or when food was short.

1485 late in the Summer bought its own uncertainties, the weather although warm in August had turned wet and many floods were about the county and many lanes were covered in deep water.

This made getting to market in Redemoor troublesome, and despite the narrow-wheeled cart and horse being able at getting through a mire, as the wheels were narrow and cut into the mud and filth, it nevertheless did strain the slower horse.

Carltonstone was a trivial place, a hamlet of 30 or so villains they worked a handful of small perches of land, where roots and beans were grown, pigs were kept, and some sheep were grazed.

It was an unusual quiet place joined in the cleft of small villages close to its narrow lanes where stone, the pale blue creamy Carlton stone was taken for the erecting of cottages and buildings in the village as well as being sold further afield.

The village was blessed with a small chapel, a simple wooden construction with a squared tower holding the bell and set on a Carltonstone plinth, an ancient plot, on a place which over the century's had had a place of worship. At this time this was a wholly Christian community, the church (a chapel) became and was the centre of community life, not just for practising faith, but the hub of the locality where news from afar would be given by the priest or vicar, as he would have heard the latest news on law and taxes or alms and the developments on-going in the war of the roses in close by Leicester and Nottingham and across certain parts of the north east.

A blacksmith, wheelwright, a saddler, and a capper worked in the linier hamlet, a collection of small cottages and half stone built, two roomed places with nothing resembling a garden just a basic place to live, many parishioners were simple folk eking out a simple life with skills passed on from generation to generation, such as saddlers and cappers (leather cap makers) linen and lace socks and stockings. They worked in hovel like conditions dim light and long, long days.

A bonnet maker and lace weaver; traded their wares in the local market, the village was built on a hill close to a main route of roman roads, fed by crisscross routes of drovers tracks and verge ways and a main lane. Although it was a quiet backwater it had a thriving trade from passers-by.

The villagers were of the firm belief that time was for working, worshiping, or sleeping, life was hard, toil was unforgiving. Food basic gruel and stews were the main staples, good food wasn't an option of choice they lived by foraging, bartering, or selling what they could make or gather.

Many folks here suffered a harder life, cold winters, and short growing periods, any man or women were destined not to see their 50th or even 40th birthday, many perished in the long winters of the previous two years, in 1484 and 1483 the winters were hard and where the wind howled, and the snow came deep, harsh, and cruel.

Some died from the cold, disease, infection, and pests. Some survived and lived good lives, but only a few. It was expected in any family that some siblings wouldn't survive, and by the hand of God who was merciful in his choice some would continue in this world.

Within the village was a blacksmithy, an open yard which was gated on three sides, a roar of an open large fire in a stone pit, fuelled by wood cut from the nearby wooded lands and forests next to the river Mease in the hollow, not a far walk, the smoke from the smithy hung in the air on still days and blew afar to Redemoor, which was a long mile away, on those regular breezy days.

This Irenmonger's (Blacksmith's yard) was a place where horses could be shod, the horse-shoes circa 1400's – 1500's were a thin iron shoe with a leather under pad, a feature of the locality and place they came from in deepest rural Leicestershire, felloes and spokes for cart-wheels could be replaced and were fitted in the blacksmiths yard.

The smith would make useful implements these were handmade and worked together by the "Irenmonger" 'Jervis and assisted by his brother Thomas'.

Thomas was a fletcher and bodkin maker, a wood turner and felly smith. His work was made up of long days, making arrows and fletching them, his training however, was in the heavier work of wheelwrighting.

This wasn't a business of as we would know it today, but a way of life it was the only work he had even known. Long days during the summer and short days in the winter.

Thomas missed his father and uncle, but he appreciated working today and every day with his older brother Jervis.

Jervis had learnt his craft and trade from his father Matthew, it was a long apprenticeship, from the age of 10 Jervis was working with his father learning the styles and skills needed to take the oath of a blacksmith it was a hard apprenticeship, his father was a hard taskmaster.

Jervis was skilled in smelting his own Iron from stone quarried in nearby Mancetter and Gresley to the north. Jervis was the elder of the two brothers, his own Father and Uncle were brothers who worked together for 26 hard years, until the death of Mathew who suffered and died with scrofula, "mal du roi" or the "King's Evil". The smoke from the forge was partly to blame, and the family blamed the evils in the smoke, but it was a common Tuberculosis that saw him to his eventual long suffocating death at the age of 47.

Thomas's uncle William died three years after when as they were repairing the axle on a large hay cart, unexpectantly and without warning, it toppled over and fell on him, crushing his chest breaking his arm, it happened in the lane outside the yard, he died in great pain from broken ribs punctured lung and other Injuries.

In the short time before he died, and before a ravaging pneumonia set in, he instructed Jervis and Thomas to carry on the yard to support his widow and their mother.

The brothers did carry on as their father had instructed, they worked together sharing the forge and yard and had done so since they were young men just out of their apprenticeships.

The best of yards was thought to be a fletcher and blacksmith working together and was a good union of brothers, smithing, craft and craftsmen, this was a valuate combination of skill and was considered to be useful when the country or county was at war.

Thomas the Turner and Jervis the Smith were their known names in nearby Redemoor and Barleystone.

Thomas made good stout staffs and staves, his arrows were known as to be the straightest in the county, the combination of Jervis's hardened bodkins and crescent heads made for excellent hunting arrows for the best of archers, bowmen, and hunters.

He was a talented leather worker, wood turner and fettler, his bowls, platters, and spoons were much sought after in the locality and were popular with people passing through the markets in Redemoor each week.

Thomas made leather tabards, a simple form of armour which protected the wearer from attack of robbers and thieves who stalked travellers along the narrow local lanes.

Jervis's wife made long leather coats and capes with attractive riveting and fine stitching's. Hats and caps and belonging bags of leather and tanned felts, she bargained these from the slaughters and feltings in Atherstone and Witherlyvale, it was here where the river flooded and the Mythe and marshes there, made for good curing of the hides in large oak and nettle infused drenches and pits, where the tannins in the nettles, Lyme, Elm and Oak bark was soaked into them to make them supple workable hides.

Clara preferred the summer pig leather hides as they were generally more supple to work with, this in turn bought them a premium price at market as they were softer and offered wearer more comfort. She would occasionally repair field boots (feld booties) using this softer leather lining the boot with hessian and old shirts.

Jervis's wife's coats were long tied at the middle with a lash catch and a belt, they were popular locally, Jervis and his wife Clara would use the late evenings in the summer to make them up in readiness for the onset of winter. They were popular, local villagers and some from afar would come to the market in Redemoor to buy them or they would swap them for other simple goods and or tools.

Visitors to the market usually travelled from Stapleton, Desford, Hinckley, Ibstock and as far as the garrison town of Tamworth. Market goers would buy Thomas's arrows, spoons and dishes, square platters, drinking cups and pots, staves, and pokes, that he had faddled and turned from local wood collected from local woods and coppices.

He was skilled in using a pole treadle to turn them. It was hard work on the shoulders and hands, Thomas could make staffs and poles from oak and elm, it was useful work and bought in a steady penny more for his speciality which was hunting arrows.

Jervis made the best quality bodkins in Leicestershire, they were hardened, true and perfectly accurate.

They sold the meat of venison, pigeons, crows' rooks, and rabbits from the yard in Carltonstone or from the back of the cart on market days in Redemoor. Whenever they could take a kill, they would, rich meat was scarce.

The best joints of the carcass went to the manor house located on the outskirts of the village, the rest would be divided up for selling or consumption in the extended family from a good boiling pot, which was in most homes, a pot of stew or hot pot kept cooking for days even weeks, as the pot became low on ingredients, more would be added with ale and goats milk mainly root vegetables and pigeon, cuts of pig and wild boar, rabbit and small birds were popular and readily available..

It wasn't the best of flavours in comparison to our commercially produced food of today, but it was wholesome and a good meal to be had after a hard day in the smithy's yard.

Thomas and Jervis would share the boar too, a late summer slaughter of the wild boar bought good food for the winter times.

A Christmas time slaughter saw them through the harsh howl and darkness of the wintertime and through the winter solstice into spring.

Often the wives and women from the village would ask Jervis to cook bread or bake parsnips carrots in pots, or a stew to simmer in the embers of the forges fire.

Thomas had a wife, Anna, she was in her late twenties slim with long red hair, a paled complexion, she had green eyes, she was a mother of three, two boys and a girl, she was devoted to Thomas and had settled into the village life since meeting Thomas in Hinckley livestock market 10 years before.

Anna was a fieldworker (feldworker) she would tend the crops on the perches at the back of the small cottage, it was a small holding but productive in the spring and summer months.

The cottage she shared with Thomas was stone built on the ground from local Carlton stone, up to about a man's head height, there after it was timbered and topped with a tumbling chaotic thatch roof.

Thomas, Anna and the three children lived there, the cottage was cool in the summers and bitterly cold in the winters. Bed coverings were exchanged and bargained in the Redemoor market held each midweek, and on a Saturday morning.

These would give warmth for the children as bed coverings and Thomas and Anna as they shared a bed upstairs from the stable beneath the cottage where the benefit of the warmth of the animals below would take the chill of the coldest of nights.

One early morning in late summer, Jervis was making the fire in the smithy yard, as he used the foot treadled heart shaped bellows made of leather and wood to feed the fire with regular puff of air, he had placed logs on it, the crackle and popping of the green wood as it started to burn could be heard from across Green lane, a curl of pale smoke rose from the fire hearth engulfing the yard and surrounding cottages.

"that is an early morning welcome smell" said Thomas waving the smoke away from his face as he crossed the lane over to the yard, "It is" said Jervis, "good day to thee broth'r" said Thomas "and a fair one to thee too" said Jervis, "is all well"?,

"It is" said Thomas "I pray there was a wind today to blow this sleep from my head and eyes" "Yes" said Jervis "I think we are looking at another hot day, Jervis chewed some sweet birch bark and held a broom under one arm. "Brother" he said to Thomas.

" The well needs to be covered, Jervis pointed across to the well opposite with his broom, "some in the village forget and not of mind that pests and vermin come in the night".

"I will attend to it today" said Thomas "are we going to the mid-week market at Redemoor brother"? asked Thomas, "I am going yes are you going to join with me?" "Jervis replied "it is the midweek market and Clara has request I bring back some duck eggs," "I will be" said Thomas, "I have some dishes and platters for selling, and I want to hear the bellman's news from afar".

"That's good then we shall go and do our selling and barter together", Jervis tore at a bread and bit into a boiled duck egg Clara had left for him on his bench, he leant back and ate it as he gazed across the countryside towards the market of Redemoor and the tall spire of St Marks Church. It was going to be an unusual warm humid day in August.

Jervis pointed to the sky "It will be a warm muggy day today look at the sky Thomas, we must drink some sweet ale before we set off".

Later, Jervis bought out a horse from the shelter at the side of the yard, she was broad and stout an old girl, slow, but strong, used by the brothers for many years and stabled close to the cottage under the workshop. He offered her backing on to his cart, a smart two wheeled wagon, he made the horse back into the cart and secured he on. She was used to the routine and knew her way almost unguided to market.

On to the back of the cart Jervis loaded, a scythe, three wooden buckets, ten large knives a pocket full of small gentlemen knifes and some spoons, he had a sword, a gentleman's knife and a hand axe and a breast plate.

He put two long leather coats and some hats on the cart and covered them with a sackcloth.

He called to Thomas who had with him Jervis's son, and a selection of platters and dishes, made from elm and ash, some rough and some smoothed with stones. He with a grunt loaded several willow staffs which were always good to sell and a large basket of arrows with bodkins

"Is that all we have today?" said Jervis, "It is so said Thomas, we have more but we will not sell well today, if it is hot then bring a flagon of ale for our thirst Thomas, I have placed one with our meal.

As they started to walk the horse and cart around, Thomas passed by the stone built well, "I want to attend to the well later when it is cooler "you will need to fashion a top cover for it Thomas". "I have something in mind" he replied.

CHAPTER 2

The two men stood onto the cart, the boy settled on to the back overlooking the shoulders of his father and uncle, the horse faltered a little as the bridal and harness took up the slack as they set off, slowly they climbed village from the green towards the toll house, bidding a good day to the one or two villagers and perchers along the village to the top and turned right towards Redemoor.

The journey took a while to cover the space of a mile and a half at slow pace, they arrived Jervis and Thomas were aware of the rising heat, it was getting very warm. Jervis stood at the entrance to the market square as Thomas and his son went off to find a place for them to set up the cart.

Thomas arrived back and pointed Jervis to a good place to set up their stall, Jervis went across to see Mr Grundy the Toby, he took the shilling, then Jervis returned to unhitch the horse and walk to the back of the market with the boy, they set up their cart placing their goods on a bump of hay and blankets so to sell on the square which was near to the sheep pens.

The market was still quiet, the shadows still offered a cool refuge, as it was now very warm the air was still and quiet there seemed to be little to take a breath with.

Thomas walked off to talk to another wood turner from Shenton Lane. They discussed the availability of elm and oak wood and talked about Thomas's long staffs, the man bought one and Thomas swapped it for some money and a large round piece of planked wood, made for an odd small wheel someone previously had not returned to collect.

As the morning came on Jervis had sold a small knife and a leather flop cap, for 5 pennies he also talked to his friend who wanted a scythe sharpening and repairing, Jervis said he would collect it on his way home later that day.

The two men walked away talking to each other in the foreign tongue, laughing and joking to each other as they moved away, Thomas, noticed they had met a third man who was holding 3 pale grey horses, he was dressed the same fine clothes and hat, they slowly walked off and continued looking around the market square inspecting ducks' eggs and pheasants.

At midday there was a banging on the walls of the market stables, and the clinking of an old steel bell. There stood a man who was tall and broad, his tunic was brown, grubby, and torn, but once would have been a pink (red) there was an old posey in his lapel, some of his buttons were missing he wore long tights and odd shoes. He perused the cart and asked if Jervis had any shoes or booties, Jervis said he hadn't but Mr Buckler in the stall opposite may have, the Man thanked him and made across the square to see.

Two men approached Thomas, they had been circling the square eating young apples inspecting goods on some of the other stalls and carts, they picked up some of his arrows, each man inspected them looking closely at the fletching and the sharpness of the bodkins, "how many pennies will buy these?" Asked one of the men. They were looking at Thomas's staves and staffs, flexing them to see if they would break, these are good, are they oak, no said Thomas, willow, and these are ash. We handed them some thick poles these were a base for a axe head or a halberd or could be fashioned for a pike or a poke pole.

Thomas found it hard to understand them as they were clearly not local men. Thomas asked them to speak clearly, "How much are these pokes for a King's battle?". "Half groat" was Thomas' first bid, "cheap enough to kill an English fool do you say?" the other man asked. Thomas wasn't sure if this was a statement or a question, again he asked them to speak clearly. Thomas noticed both men were carrying knives, they looked expensive knives with handles made from horn and each sheathed in a fine leather scabbard. They also had fine hats, pheasant feathers and green brocade embellished the brim, a white tassel hung from the back of the brim, these were wealthy men from far off lands.

The men huddled and stood together," talking in a strange language, they all three turned to Thomas "how many? How many do you have?

Thomas secretly was wishing Jervis had returned as he felt a little out of his depth. Thomas said, "I have 1 gross with bodkin, and maybe one gross ready for the bodkin".

"Do you make these for my Burgundy long-bow? Thomas looked at his bow slung across his broad shoulders he guessed it was roughly the same as an English long bow "are they all one man's chest length draw"? asked the taller of the two men, "Yes", said Thomas "see here, he handed an arrow to one of the men he took his long bow from his shoulder, he offered an arrow to the bow, and pulled it back "do you have more he asked, "Well I can make more","" I will need them soon", "I see said Thomas, when will be soon?" "By one week" said the taller of the two men and you will take a half groat for each arrow?" "Yes, I will," said Thomas. "Where is your workplace fletcher? said the second man, it is a mile and a half down that track in Carltonstone. "ça peut être bon" said the man, I will visit tomorrow English. Thanks be to you said Thomas I await your visit Thomas smiled at the man.

The clothes they had were strange, not locals, they wore a leather waistcoat, a studded shirt, leather and sheepskin woollen jerkins and pantaloons, their boots were not made locally, and these were not local men thought Thomas.

He thought about how wise he had been in courting these men, but his wife was due to give another child in a few months' time, the money would be welcome.

Jervis came back and asked Thomas, "who were those men brother"? I don't know said Thomas, they wanted to buy all my arrows, Jervis asked why? There was a caution in his voice, "what use do they have for them? They do not look like hunters" said Jervis, "I don't know said Thomas, they joked about killing an English fool", Jervis said "who is an English fool Thomas"? Thomas turned and faced his brother, wiping sweat from the heat of the late morning from his brow. "Jervis you talk as if you are angry with me, why do you question me so? I didn't ask brother, I was thinking of our money, these men want 2 grosses of arrows".

I see said Jervis, to me my young brother these men look dangerous, I advise you not to take them into your confidence, my words to you are, Jervis held Thomas by his arm, "hear me brother, do not trust them or mix our business with them" they speak in a strange tongue not of these parts.

"They are coming to visit our yard tomorrow Jervis", Thomas replaced his cap, he pulled away from Jervis's grasp and pushed past him, "Why, in our lord's name Thomas?" asked Jervis, "they want the arrows and they were looking at my staves and staffs, I said a will be able to make more for them", "but we do not know these men" said Jervis "what would be your regret if they are robbers Thomas? Remember brother Thomas your arrows are good, straight, and true, they will kill men perhaps good men, I as your brother urge you, it will be wise for you must take great caution Thomas please consider my words, you will regret if you are impaled on your own spike Thomas! "Thomas was replacing platters from the cart, from one side of the cart he looked across at Jervis. "You are being too cautious brother Jervis".

Jervis scoffed at Thomas, "caution will not make harm for us brother" said Jervis, Jervis moved to Thomas's side he lifted a pale onto the back of the cart, the water was for the horse and had become warm, Jervis took a scarf from his neck, he dipped it in the luke warm water and squeezed it out wiping the back of his neck and then his brow, the weather and heat was getting worse, the air had become still and the flies were a bother to both men, Jervis slapped Thomas on the back, "come the bellman is here, let us hear his news".

On the steps of the cross in the marketplace stood a swarthy grubby man dressed in a black cloak It was a warm morning and he was dressed heavily, his odd shoes with buckles and bells and stockings were dull and dirty, he opened a large bag and from within he took out a scroll, he placed the bag at his feet and slowly unravelled the scroll placing the ribbon which held it secure on his left shoulder.

He stood still and scanned the marketplace for a while, several people were milling around, he waited and chose his moment, at the top of his voice he bellowed to the gathered crowd in front of him.

"H're ye, i calleth to thee, heareth ye, cometh hither here and heareth mine own holl'r, f'r those of redemo'r i has't news from afar"

He bellowed from the steps, Thomas was keen to hear, what the Bellman would have to say.

The man shouted with a deep voice and told of vagabonds and robbers working the roads around this parish, good folk need to be aware and armed and be forewarned. Do not take coins or chattel on your person, for fear of thieves and vagabonding. Stay off these laynes at the night!

He raised and held his hand high, his cape and cloak pulling on his long dirty frills on his wrists , he took a dower look to his face with a frown, he called for quiet,! as the news turned grim, he took a blackened cloth from his tunic, and waived it before his face, he took a darker look on to his face, he shook his head and with a deep breath announced that "death was amongst us in the form the French 'swett', a cold deathly disease, with a swift end to this life, it exudes homely misery with evil and soured vapours around the heart" Pray at the doors of your homely places the lord will be with you to prevent its entrance into your homes.

He cleared his rasped rattled voiced throat and cleared his voice. In his left hand was his stave, he waved it left to right in from of the listening crowd. People of this parish listen to my words".

"The lords are at war, the King is new to our England in only two years since his coronation, the Lords are waring in disputes and this war of the York and Lancaster continues, there are those who consider Richard the newest King is not a true King, he scanned the assembled crowd with one eye squinted, then continued "may their tongues be taken by the wilds of dogs' he shook the scroll and continued, Henry is afar but has pledged a return to these shores with armies from across the sea".

As to the truth, the family of York, the final victory of the Lancastrians in the Wars of the Roses may have seemed a tragic disaster, but Henry Tudur doeth know of the importance of the York support for his return to our land, he has promised to marry Elizabeth Duchess of Suffolk, a promise to this country and made before he lands in England. This may well have come to assist to the losses of Yorkist support for King Richard but take heed and beware,

French spies have been seen in the county of Mercia to those here assembled before me beware of their questioning.

The bellman waved his black cloth before the crowd again "be noted I bring news from the courts and Aldermen he bellowed, At Gibbet Lane not 2 long miles from here there will be a hanging, a murderer in our towyn will be put to his end at the morning time, you are called as witnesses to the end of his crime", I report to you gathered that horses have been stolen from a manor house in Orton on the hill, to much distress to the lady of the house and her husband, the vagabonds who took the 3 horses of good order they were caught in possession of the beasts on the fields around the village of Austery and were arrested in the shadow hours of the morning of a Sunday some good weeks since, these 4 men are soldiers from the Mercian Garrison at Tamworth, they have been dismissed, stripped and shamed from the Garrison and reported to the baillivis. They had been beaten down with pain in the morning and held in the gaol without chattels or coinage.

It is the wishes of the honourable Duke of Stafford, the Lord of Tamworth, that you all should know that they have been bought before the Stafford Shire's Portman moot court room, it was told to the sitting court on the Feast of

St Edith's day that these men took the beasts to sell them for profit for themselfes, they were shackled and allowed a chance to talk, and admit to other offences abided to them, including, butchery offences, receipt of stolen goods and bloodshed and exude their weak and lying pleas for mercy, then at once before the good men of the court.

These 4 men of the robbing's were then remanded in gaol and the case was sent to be heard at The Piepowder Court and easily convicted in the presence of the Lord of Tamworth of their evil thefts.

Their troubling was then bought before the View of Frankpledge, there without representation from the jury but in the presence of the Lord of Tamworth and the Duke of Stafford all of good men and Lords, it is sentenced and recorded in the roll of the courts there sitting, that they will be without mercy or further hearings of their crymes be dispatched from this gods great earth according to Mercian law, England's law and gods law for their robbing's and bloodshed and only after the hanging on M'nday next of the 24th August in the year of our lord 1485 of the villainous murderer Thomas Hundley.

They will be shown firstly to witness to Thomas Hundley his miserable hanging and eventual death of the murderer Thomas Hundley they then will face the cold punishment accorded to them.

"Those gents shall hang by the nek.
until those gents' art dead."

Their lifeless corpses will be taken from the gallows and their bodies stripped to display their guilty demeanour and tarred and left to rot and tied to the public pillory outside the curtilage of the parish of Orton on the Hill as a demonstration to good honest men of the validity of their robbing's, blood shedding and thefting.

It is advised that all men in good character and marriage and gods holy faith attend the hangings and pledge their agreement or argument to these convictions and sentences.

It is as well that every man makes cleane the
strette's before ther dorrz' and 'yt everyman
kepe ther gret dogges in ther hows sy s', to all the
assembled and those living with in the walls of
Redemoor that there is to you no exceptions.

The Bellman finished his announcement to the village of Redemoor shouting.

"H're ye, i calleth to thee, heareth ye, cometh
hither and heareth mine own holl'r, f'r
those of redemo'r in the parish and the

market lodging, I have given thee valorous news from afar" good day to you".

CHAPTER 3

It was less than common knowledge for many years after the battle that to make claim on his hold on the throne, Henry declared himself King by right of conquest from 21 August 1485, the day before Bosworth Field. So, any man who had fought for or with Richard against Henry would be guilty of a common treason and Henry could take away under Law, the lands and property of Richard III, while restoring it to his own conquered lands.

Henry spared the life of Richard's nephew and

heir, John de la Pole, the Earl of Lincoln, and in a dangerous but worthwhile move made Margaret Plantagenet to Countess of Salisbury.

He decided not to summon Parliament or address the baronages or until after his own coronation, which took place in Westminster Abbey on 30 October 1485.

Following his crowning Henry issued an edict that.

"Beffore any gentle 'man who is't sw're fealty to the King wouldst, notwithstanding any previous attaind'r, beest secureth in his prop'rty and p'rson."

The marketplace was starting to get busy it was midmorning, the Bellman cleared his throat coughing loudly with a bad halitosis and rotten teeth, spluttering and spitting over the front row of the assembled crowd.

He used his grubby sleeve of his heavy coat to wipe his mouth, he stood down, he rolled the scroll up, he took the brown ribbon from his shoulder he carefully tied it to the scroll, his eyes squinted as he scanned the crowd, as he did, he placed the scroll carefully in his bag, he stood up and stretched his back.

He picked up his bag and walked slowly with a long stride kicking up dry filth as he strolled across the cobbles of the square, he removed his hat and bowed to a woman and her son, he put the black cloth into his hat and replaced it on his head, he walked slowly to the middle marketplace square, he looked around he took some snuff from a small cloth bag on his wrist, he reached up to place a handwritten notice on the wooden post there.

Thomas returned to where the cart was, Jervis was standing waiting for him to return, as he approached Jervis didn't ask about the Bellman's address to the crowd, he had made enough of it to understand the content and was quite unimpressed.

"So, brother Thomas" said Jervis leaning on his shoulder and whispering in his ear," beware of those men they could be French spies", Jervis chuckled and laughed. Thomas was not in any mood for joking.

"I will not listen to your story of fears Jervis, this is a good day for selling our wares, if they pay us, it will be a good day's work. I will be occupied well for the next market. You should be pleased Jervis". "I am Brother, I am also wary of strangers, and those from foreign lands, as you should be, that is all, you heard well what the bellman said.

"We will be satisfied tomorrow I am sure of this Jervis, I will need bodkins Brother, bright and with a sharp end". "I know you will be" said Jervis "and as you are my brother, I will let you have them at a price which is as keen as the sharpest points on my bodkins. Just please be careful these are not good men.

The two brothers continued to sell into the afternoon, they ate meat, rabbit and mutton and sharp apples and bread for a mid-day meal together. Later Jervis took a meal to his son who was sitting with the horse in the field at the back of the market square, the field was yellow and covered with clover, the horse was under a tree sheltering from the suns heat.

Jervis had taken the pale, fetch some water for the horse said Jervis, the boy took the pale to the nearby stream, he filled it then walked back to his father, he placed the bucket next to the horse, the horse lent forward and lapped the water furiously,

The young boy sat next to the horse, "father when will we be going back home? it is a very warm day I am in need of homely water father", he asked, Jervis looked across the fields toward Wells on the hill, the view was clear but across the hills at Merevale, in the distance Jervis could see that stormy clouds were approaching across the vale, he said "wait for a while eat your meal, then harness up and bring the mare to us, I will tell your uncle, we will get ready to beat that storm down the hill".

Jervis left the boy eating his apples and curds and a dry cobble of bread, he returned to the marketplace to find two more strangers talking to Thomas, this time Thomas made a sale of two dozen arrows each, monies had been exchanged and Thomas was pleased, Jervis had sold another bucket and a scythe. "Jervis" Thomas cheered, "we have done well today", "yes Thomas, but we must go, we cannot stay long Thomas there is a dark storm approaching, I told the boy to bring the mare to us, we must make for home and shelter soon".

"Oh" Thomas said as he looked west across the fields at the dark clouds, the sky was ominously dark and threatening ,they loaded the cart up, the boy trotted the mare into the square and the men and boy after putting the horse in harness made for home, the horse and cart made an easy way down the Barton track and up again into Carltonstone, part way along the track where the track crossed the wooden bridge across the river Mease they looked to the west and in the corner of the woods were two tents, conical in shape with dark grey and green covers over their tops, there was a fire smoking softly and the smoke rising up through the dense canopy of green Oaks, Ash and Elms.

The tents were well made and two men with their horses were standing by leaning on long staffs. Jervis said "are those the men who spoke to you in the market this morning?

Where said Thomas, Jervis pointed and said, "look to the trees, that may be your new friends". "Please do not taunt me Jervis" said Thomas, "they are not my friends, but I will take their money in a friendly manner in exchange for my wares should they approach me and offer their custom".

Thomas shook the reins and the horse carried on, "Well, let us be wary and careful brother", Jervis warned again. They continued up the hill and past the toll house into the village. The skies were increasingly darkened, the warm breeze was getting up, they unhitched the cart, and the horse was led away by the boy and the cart returned with Thomas and Jervis giving it a push to the side of the forge.

Thomas went in his cottage to greet his wife, she bid him a "good afternoon Thomas "She greeted him with a kiss and gave him a drink of well water and apple juices and a cut of curds with some bread and honey, she had been making a cheese from the goat's milk.

The room was full of wasps buzzing around the food, Anna asked Thomas to rid the house of these wasps" these jaspers scare the children and are getting aggressive with me they have been getting boozed on the Plumbs in the orchard we need rid of them Thomas "she said, " I will deal with them later today" he said, it would be wise to leave the shutters open Anna these beasts can fly away, they don't like the smoke from the fire and I will burn some green branches from the willow tree that will send them on their way". .

"It is warm today" he said, then looking around he asked "where are the children? Anna said, "They are in the fields down below collecting berries Thomas why"? "I must ask you to keep them close to home and in sight Anna for the next few days, there are visitors from afar in the area and I and Jervis think we need to take care".

"I see she said, I will go and get them in a while", "no, Anna, please go and get them now, there is a storm coming. It had already started to darken; the warm wind was getting stronger; in the distance some rumbles of thunder were rolling around the vale and they could hear that the storm was approaching.

Thomas closed the doors he pulled the horse into the stable below the workshop next to the cottage, Anna ran to get the children, as she got to the top of the meadow, she could hear them and see them screaming in fear of the thunder as they ran back towards her. They ran through the long grass holding their petty coats aprons up as the berries tumbled out, don't run Anna called to them, take you time in the long grass or you will fall.

She noticed a man in dark clothes walking along the riverbank, he appeared to have a dark menacing face, she had never seen him before she was sure he was not a local man. "Come children run home before the storm gets us wetted" the children were breathless but walked with Anna back to the cottage, as she approached the back of green lane, she looked over her shoulder and saw the man looking back at her, she hurried back to the cottage and through the back of the small perch of land where she was growing swede and turnip a small crop of barley and some peas. She closed the wicker fence gate and secured it, she looked across the fields down to the river again, she stood back and looked along the whole length of the riverbank, but the man had gone.

The rain storm started slowly it was going to be a heavy storm, Anna could tell, as the speed of the rain drops were heavy and slowly increased, then the rain turned in an instant to hail, it came fast and heavy the children just made it made it into the home, the Green lane outside the cottage soon turned white with a layer of ice cold hailstones, as quick as the hail started;

a flash of lightening lit up the small room and was followed quickly by a clap of thunder, the deep rumble shook the cottage, Thomas could feel it through his feet, the horse was startled and reared up and pulled against her post.

Thomas heard her and went into the low roofed stable to ease the mare and settle her, as fast as he did another flash and crash of thunder shook the cottage walls, then the rain came heavy, roaring on the roof thatch and wooden roof slats, the intense downpouring soon a stream was forming in the lane outside Thomas's and Jervis's cottages, washing mud and filth down the lane into a large pool.

Jervis had stayed out in the forge covering the cart and the fire to stop it being extinguished by the rain. The sky was black and low on the hills, thunder and lightning was loud and ferocious and by now overhead. It was going to be an afternoon of storm, this was a bad thing for the forge, Jervis cursed the sky and storm as he fought to keep the fire going in the forge.

Thomas said to Anna we haven't seen a storm like this for many years, Anna said I know look at the roof of the yard, as they looked across the road the water was coming off the roof like a waterfall, Jervis had taken shelter in the lean too shack in the yard, he sat there trying to lite his fire the few embers still glowing in the forges fire grate, as the storm raged outside the wind was swirling around and blowing leaves off the tree's at the back of the forges yard,

The water was streaming into the front of the yard and in a few moments had washed stones and soil into the yard entrance. Jervis was piling wood on the top of the fire he loaded kindling in big piles to try and encourage the fire to keep alight.

He knelt on one knee to pushing fistfuls of kindling and brush into the fire grate, it felt to Jervis that he was fighting a losing battle against the rage of the rain and storm outside.

A huge swathe of smoke was coming from the fire grate but little flame, Jervis took a large sheet of cloth and put it in the water bucket close by, he them covered the fire by a half, this made the air draw up into the fire centre and amidst the roar of the air passing through the pile of charcoal and coke soon bought flames and the sound of the hearth changed, flames crept round the back of the fire grate, Jervis removed the wetted cloth sheet and folded it up, he watched the fire grow and in a few minutes settled, he could feel the heat on his face, he reached for wooded logs and branches and placed then carefully on top of the roaring fire, he put lots of charcoal on top and stood back. He was satisfied the fire was alive, he gathered more charcoal from his store.

Jervis looked across the lane, the rain was heavy it was flooding the lane in great lakes and the water rushed down the track washing and swirling mud and stones into the front of the forge and yard. The thunder was still cracking and rumbling overhead, the wind had dropped to a hot breeze, and the storm was passing by, but very slowly.

Jervis spotted something out of the corner of his eye across the lane at Thomas's home, It was Thomas waving at him to come across, Jervis held his hand up and gestured that he was fine. He was busy with the fire and some clearing up. The storm continued well into the late evening, the flooding in the lane started to drain away, it left behind a thick sticky mud. The few horses that past the forge had churned up the mud and the track was almost impassable on foot. The sky remained dark and gloomy; clouds were swirling under the rain clouds.

Jervis had returned to his home late in the evening, his wife Clara was waiting for him with a meal of vegetable stew with a portion of mutton, Jervis said "hello" quietly, not to disturb the boy she said.

He sat with Clara as he ate, it was darkened the light was fading fast now and he sat and ate by candlelight, Clara told him of her news, she said "the storm must have tired the boy as he was sleeping peacefully", Jervis said "thanks be to God the storm had passed", he couldn't recall a storm of such ferocious intent as this day's storm.

Clara said she really scared and was concerned for his wellbeing whilst he was in the forge, Jervis reminded her that keeping the fire a light was important as the fire was their lively hood. This weather was unusual.

Jervis finished his meal, he looked across to the forge, he could see the glow of the fire against the back wall of the yard. He told Clara he would be back in a short while; he was going to load the fire once more before his bed. Clara said she would wait for him but would check on the boy and get ready for his return.

CHAPTER 4

Jervis took a lantern and walked through the mud and filth in the lane, he made his way to the yard of the forge, in the shadows and against the flicker of the lanterns light he saw a man standing next to the fire. "Hey", he called, the man looked around, "what are you doing here?" Jervis moved closer through the wooden gate but not too close, "I am at your mercy" said the man, "and why is that?" said Jervis, The man didn't reply, he just stood there, Jervis noticed his clothes were steaming and his clothes and cloak were wet, "I asked you what you are doing and what do you want", "I am Sir just warming my arms the weather had soaked my cloak and my horse is startled by the storm", I see said Jervis, "who are you?"

"My name is Richard Sharnford, I am an honourable man Sir, just wanting some warmth for a moment Sir, Im sorry I did not intend to trespass here" Jervis said, "have you taken a meal this evening time Richard?" "No, I have not" said Richard, you will wait there until I return said Jervis, Jervis made his way to his home a few steps away, he gathered a bowl of warm stew from the hearth in to one of Thomas's deep wooded bowls, he walked back across the lane quickly in a short while, the stranger Richard was still there, his horse tied up to the wooden fence posts.

Here Richard, he held out the simple bowl and warm food, The man stood aback, im obliged to you said the stranger, this is a gift on such a bad stormed day", Jervis stood on the other side of the fire, which was now crackling and spitting "It may be"! said Jervis, "but if you are honourable you will take it as kindness and politely and in return you will offer a favour", Jervis pointed his finger at the bowl, "Sir, eat your meal before it gets too cold to be tasty and savoured" Jervis instructed him.

The man took a few mouthfuls of the stew and warm broth, he swallowed it gladly, and asked Jervis "what favour do you seek Sir?" Jervis was loading more wood on to this forge fire, he covered the next layer with local coal and some strips of peat. He stood back as a curl of heavy smoke rose from the hearth.

The flickering lantern made the man's dark face features hard to read, Jervis looked the man up and down, where do you come from?" asked Jervis, "I am from Leicester assises Sir", "and what brings you this way?" Jervis enquired, "I am on the lookout for spies and robbers reported in this parish".

"I see" said Jervis, Richard Sharnford, "I will tell you, there are no chattels here of any worth or note, I am a simple blacksmith, this is my yard, you are welcome to shelter here this night, on condition you keep my fire in this hearth alight".

"There is kindling and fresh wood over there, there is coal and burning sod here. All I ask is that from time to time you put fuel on my fire, This is in return for some shelter and is what I ask of you in a favour".

The man was finishing up his meal, he put the bowl down on a table, he stood back and offered a handshake to Jervis,

As they shook hands the stranger said "Sir, I am here also for the hanging of a murderer on Monday at dawn I am here to assert his miserable soul to the lord or the flames of hell as he will be judged. I see Jervis replied, "are you a hangman"? ", "No Sir I am the Kings witness, Alderman and the county sheriff".

Jervis turned and looked at the mans features in the flickering red shadows "well that may be your business Sir, it is my business to shoe horses and make the sharpest bodkins to sell and to feed my family".

Jervis put some blankets at the man's feet, he stood up and looked the man in the eye with confidence. Jervis continued "Without a hot fire I can do neither Richard Sharnford"

The stranger looked back "Sir, I will maintain your flames and fire and thank you for your hospitality this night". Jervis shook his hand "we have an agreement Sir?" said the man "and again I am obliged to you Sir".

Richard Sharnford bowed his head and removed his Cap, Jervis took another Lantern and lit it from the hearth, "please extinguish this before you retire", I will and thanks to you Sir, Jervis made his way to the gate of the yard he picked up the empty bowl, he looked back, Richard Sharnford was looking at him, "I will break the fast with you in the morning". "Thank you again" Richard said. "Sleep well, you may rest your horse in the yard Mr Sharnford.

Jervis made his way back home, His wife Clara was anxious and asked Jervis what the delay was, Jervis explained about Richard Sharnford, Clara asked "Is that wise Jervis? you do not know this man. He may take your confidence and act badly with it. Jervis you do not know this man" she continued.

"I do now" said Jervis let us now sleep, how is the boy"? "Jervis, the boy is sleeping sound, but our son is showing a fever" said Clara, "I have mopped his brow with cool waters, he is resting now." Jervis looked in on the child he felt the back of the boys' neck, it was warm, but it was a warm close muggy night following the rainstorm earlier. "Does he have wheals or legions?" Asked Jervis, "no" Clara replied, "he is just with a summers fever, he will sleep it off I am certain."

Jervis opened the shutters in the room, the cooler air rushed in, and it was fresher than the cottage air. "Leave these shutters open" Jervis said to Clara, "come you need to rest" said Clara, "let us retire."

Jervis took a last view of the forge across the

lane; he could see the glow from the fire and the horse Richard Sharnford was riding was now inside the yard. He closed one of the shutters and took to his bed, it had been a long day, one with news from afar, strangers in the villages and foreboding of events yet to play out in the days to come. Jervis, although had a busy mind his body needed rest and he was soon sleeping fast.

During the night Jervis was woken by the voice of the boy , shouting and screaming his word were a mumble he was soon at the boys bed-side, his was writhing and grinding his teeth, Jervis shook him to wake him up but the boy remained asleep, Clara arrived concerned and asking Jervis what could they do, "We have to cool the boy "he said "get some cool water", Clara ran down the steps to the lower stable where the well head was, she lifted a pale of fresh water, filled a jug and took a cloth from the fire crate which was warm and dry from the fire therein.

She rushed up to Jervis and the boy, Jervis held the boy in his arms, Clara mopped his head and neck mopping his body down, the boy was very warm his cheeks were red, and his body covered in a rash, "my god my god" repeated Clara.

"Please don't, I know you are concerned but don't wish the worse" said Jervis, "the boy is strong this is a summer fever you said it was a summer fever Clara"," I pray to god this is a fever Jervis, let me hold him", Jervis handed over the boys limp body to Clara's arms, she huddled him close Jervis went down the stairs to refill the jug with cooler water and returned, He continued to mop the boy's body letting the water soak the boys back and hair.

After some time, the boy seemed to have cooled a little and he was breathing better and softly, Clara stripped his bed and placed him on top of fresh bed clothes she had stripped him to let the humid but cool air of the early morning to cool him further, she returned to Jervis who was now sleeping deeply. She stepped in beside him, he put his arm around her and held onto each other quietly praying for the boy, they both listened to the boys breathing, drifting off to sleep.

It continued to be an uncomfortable and humid warm night, the rain outside had abated for a while, but the air was muggy, and the soil wet underfoot.

The following morning Jervis took from his bed at dawn, he opened the shutters in the room below, there was a low mist over the land, the air was cooler than the previous few hours, the light across the countryside was still and pale blue, He checked in on his son sleeping close by. He was still warm but awake and with a croaked voice gave a "good morn" to his Father.

Come boy work will rid you of this fever", Clara called to Jervis food is on the table Jervis please come to eat.

The morning was cooler for the boy, but as Jervis was listening to the birdsong, he was expecting it to get warm, the air was heavy still and low clouds filled the skies all around. Jervis looked across to the riverbanks it was a field of wet long grasses troddled to the ground, bed of reeds swayed over with the weight of the rain on their flower heads and long stalks.

By a tree Jervis could see a figure stood half behind a tree. The man just stood there, he seemed to be looking back and as Jervis looked his eyes still getting used to the early light looking, he was directly staring at Jervis.

Clara who is that man over there? "I do not know Jervis, he has been seen on occasion by me and my neighbours", "I see" said Jervis "he is not a local, is he?", "I do not think he is" replied Clara.

Jervis took two apples and some curds and bread, in a bowl, he bid morning to Clara with a kiss on her cheek and made his way into the lane, his eyes immediately took to the forge and the gate, two tall men stood there talking to

Richard Sharnford.

Jervis arrived and placed the bowls down on the bench, "Good Morning to you", Richard Sharnford was standing close to the other two men, "Good Morning Jervis Smith these two gentlemen are looking for your brother".

"I see" said Jervis, he recognised the two men from the market the day before, "Richard do you know these men?" Jervis asked, "I do not know these gentlemen "replied Richard Sharnford, "they tell me you and your brother made a promise to sell them arrows with bodkins 1 gross according to this man". Richard raised his eyebrows and winked at Jervis.

The taller of the two men looked at Jervis, "I see your brother yesterday the day before" he said in broken English tongue. "I remember my brother telling me of your interest in his arrows," he will be here shortly!" said Jervis, Jervis picked up a bowl and handed it to Richard saying "Richard, I have bought you sustenance for your start to the day". "Again, I am in your debt Sir", said Richard Sharnford, "you have not disappointed the fire looks healthy" replied Jervis.

One of the men impatiently asked "English, when your brother will be here"? "I Have already told you he will be here shortly, I told you for the last time!", Jervis stopped in his tracks making it clear and with a fixed gaze, "tell me Sir, said Jervis, "why do you need so many Arrows?" Each of the men looked at each other, the smaller of the two said "we have a fight, and we need good straight arrows", Jervis looked the smaller man, he asked him "where do you come from?" he replied with "we are travelling through this county on our way back home to Burgundy " " I see said Jervis said "arrows kill souls do they not sir?", the tallest of the men stared back at Jervis, and who is this fight with?", Richard asked "it is with a failed King" said the other man, smirking and smiling as he said it.

"And who is the failed King? "Richard asked again, "Richard of York of course" said the other man, "Ah well" said Jervis "the arrows are sold, im sorry".

"Sold?" said the smaller of the two men, "how do you sell our arrows?" "That is for me to say" said Jervis, the taller of the foreign men stepped forward "I take you now,!" he said half drawing his dagger, Richard Sharnford moved in closer and gestured for the Frenchman to take his hand off his weapon the Frenchman spoke in another tongue to his companion, they both turned and walked into the lane, the rain had started to fall again, they mounted their horses and cantered through the mud and filth away, one of the men turned on his horse and shouted "Anglaise man, Célébrez le nouveau roi, il sera le vainqueur Viva Henry Viva Enri Tudor viva la King viva la 'Enri Tudor".

Richard said to Jervis, "let them go, they are vagabonds and probably spies from over the sea, these are not Leicestershire men, Richard ate as he spoke chewing on the bread "what is more of my concern is that they look like spies to me, if this breakfast was unwelcome Jervis, we could have challenged them" but I say to you my belly comes first.,

Jervis laughed and was poking the fire in the forge, "no" said Jervis these men have been around our village for several days now, time to see them gone",

 "Wise", replied Richard, biting into his big loaf of chewy sour dough bread and curd cheese with a hard viciously tough crust.

"Richard So thank you for your food and drink I will appreciate it, but it is now time to make my way". Richard smiled appreciatively back to Richard, "You are welcome Sir and thanks to you for keeping the forge a flame, it will allow me and my brother to have productive days in the yard even in this bad weather".

Richard lay his dark red cloak across the back of his black horse, he added his bags to the side, rolled his narrow and thin bedding into his roll and set it at the rear of his saddle.

Jervis asked him where he was staying this night, Richard said he was due to hold inspections at the Cock Inn at Sibson, he said he was acquainted with the owner, so some sustenance and a bed for the night would be possible, he said the next time he would pass by this way was on Tuesday, Jervis assured him he would be welcome in the yard if he was disappointed at the Inn, "that's kind of you Jervis, I wish you well and thank you for the food", Richard offered some coins, Jervis reminded him of is favour last night and that there was no payment.

The two men bid each other good day and gods blessings and at that Richard mounted his horse and slowly rode off in the direction of Barton as again unabated the rain was getting heavier.

CHAPTER 5

Richard Sharnford

The weather was begging to be unkind, and the rain had wetted all around again, Jervis hoisted some large canvas covers across the top of the yard he needed to work in the start of the week and shield the fire from the wet.

Thomas had arrived carrying arrows in a basket.

"So, brother you're here at last?" said Jervis, "yes, I was consoling Anna, why? quizzeled Jervis, "her cousin in Barleystone passed yesterday", "really?" said Jervis "and how had she expired?" "She had a summer sweating she died within the day," said Thomas. "That hot weather yesterday and the thunderstorms may have sent her" "foul vapours the Bellman told us, said Jervis, "yes brother, I am aware of his advice," said Thomas.

Jervis replied, "my boy is warm and was sweating last night Clara tells me it is a summer fever", Jervis pointed to the boy, the boy was sat on a seat in the yard looking pale his head in his hands and struggling for breath, "he still looks unwell" said Thomas, "some good work will stop his ills" said Jervis, "but not today" said Thomas, "he should be indoors and in a sick bed, this weather will weaken him more Jervis" "I ask you to send the boy back to your wife to take good care of him". Jervis looked to the boy and called to him, "Boy! Come here", the boy faltered and walked toward his father, he was coughing, and looking pale and weak the boy said "yes father", "Son you are not well go back to your mother she will see you well today", "yes father", the boy started to cough and spluttered, he vomited and fell to the ground, Thomas lifted him, Jervis picked him from Thomas and took him across to Jervis and Clara's cottage.

He kicked the small door open and carried the boy up the bedroom, Clara he called "the boy is sick again he is burning in heat again", Clara appeared, "oh my god please no" she shouted "my boy" she cried, Jervis placed him on the bed, the boy was delirious and his eyes were rolled back and his was dribbling, and covered in vomit, "leave him here with me Jervis", Clara asked for water and some new cloths from in front of the fire, Jervis rushed down and was back quickly with a fresh jug and some rags, Clara had stripped the boy's body again and had him laid onto the basic bed.

Clara in a whisper said, "husband be away with you leave the boy with me", Jervis clasping his hands backed out of the room, he closed the door behind him quietly, he went down to the yard washed his hands off in a bucket and called Thomas across to the well.

Thomas had taken the wooden planked wheel he bartered at the Redemoor market and rolled it to the wellhead, Jervis helped him lift it on to the top of the open well, "it is a good fit, it is a perfect roundness you have a good eye," said

Jervis.

"I will fashion a rope to secure it and make it easy to lift" said Jervis keeping an eye on the cottage, that's good" said Thomas, we need to get ready for work today, yes said Jervis. I will see you in the yard in a while, Jervis returned to the yard and secured the gate.

There waiting for him was the vicar of St Michaels Chapel, they greeted each other, "Are you well Jervis, I am sorry for sheltering in your yard but his rain is a curse this morning", "I am well, and you are welcome to the shelter, I am pleased to see you, I am troubled as my son is not well and suffering a fever, The priest took Jervis's arm, he shook his hands and looked deeply at Jervis beneath his white bushy eyebrows.

Jervis said to the reverend "please say a prayer for my boy, where is he?" asked the vicar looking around the yard expecting the boy to be close by, "he is with Clara and unwell father, we are hoping it is a summer fever, but the boy is very unwell, we are asking for gods mercy."

Thomas saw the close exchange between the two men. He thought nothing of it, he continued to work on the well top. Trying to listen to the exchange between the men.

Jervis said to the priest, "I listened to the bellman in Redemoor yesterday he warned of a French swett, I have prayed to the lord that my boy isn't with this swett father I do fer for the worst outcome", the priest turned to Jervis and put his hand on his shoulder, the boy is strong Jervis Smith, he will be in Gods good hands.

"I wish for this to be so Father " Jervis was holding back his tears, "I will continue to offer my prayers to the lord in a hope he will recover soon. Peter stroked his long white beard, "Jervis you must not be so concerned, I am sure Clara will bring his health back and he will be stronger for it. He shook off his wet cloak, "There is no French swett in these parts I am sure of it".

"While you are here father, the bellman warned of warring times ahead, what do you tell reverend?" "this may be true Jervis, the houses of York and Lancaster still are in disagreement after all these years, they are rounding up soldiers as we speak my friend, please do not appeal for either side, it is for gods will and the fate of our nation to be decided, keep you and your family safe Jervis", "I will reverend" said Jervis, he held him by the arm, the vicar said in a breathless way "you are a good man Jervis just like your father" your boy will be the same , strong and honest of nature".

Jervis dismissed his compliment and asked,

"what news do you have then, why are they here in this county?"

"I have heard that King Richard is in Nottingham and will be moving with his Northumberland armies with him to Leicester and may be even today, it is said that the Duke of Richmond Henry Tudur is in Shrewsbury and heading towards these parts along the roman way to find a battleground. Henry Tudur and the King Richard are mortal enemies and will defend their courts to the death. This may be all rumour and romance but be heeded and take the greatest of care Jervis".

The vicar coughed and faltered, he was old and frail and man of the cloth and had never taken hard toil. Jervis held him up then offered him a settle in the yard, the priest pushed him away and made his way leaning on his staff in the direction of the small church lower further down in the village. He said nothing, Jervis bid him good day, the priest walked slowly away holding his arm up as he made off.

Thomas came back with Anna to Jervis and said "what do you make of his words Jervis", Jervis said "let us not speak now Thomas, come to the forge, and bring some food we will have a brotherly discussion whilst we work" said Jervis, Anna looked concerned "Jervis what is there to debate?" asked Thomas.

"Not now Thomas please, I don't want your wife to hear this news you can tell her later today, come to the forge and we can talk". Jervis looked concerned, the worry of his son was clear to see, Thomas and Anna made their way toward their cottage as the rain started again to fall. Jervis made his way to the cottage, he called to Clara, "Clara how is our son"? "he is the same Jervis, but settled again". Jervis called up to Clara "You have done him well, I have spoken to the priest, he is praying for the boy".

"That is all we can do Jervis she said, go about your work I will call for you if the boy is unwell again," I will be Back later on" said Jervis "my love to you both", Jervis collected some things and made his way to the forge and the yard, he had a jug of ale and some cheese curd and apple sauce, a regular meal for a forgemen. He could see Thomas getting ready to join him.

After a while, the village fell silent, again the weather was hushed and still, the birds were quiet and apart from a dog barking far off, the village was quiet people had closed the shutters and closed the doors, the clouds were forming overhead, and the dark rain clouds were making their way east across the Merevale flats towards Redemoor and Carltonstone.

A warm air was apparent, and the rain started spit spot heavy raindrops and they fell from the skies with force and determination. Thomas arrived with his food and ale, more water through the village said Thomas, yes let us seal the gates of the yard said Jervis to prevent the water from flooding the forge and putting the fire out for the second time in two days, Jervis found some big stones at the back of the forge.

Thomas dragged them across the dirt floor and set them against the wooden gate then rolled up a large cloth and lay it next to the gate a closed the gate onto it and then rolled the large stones to hold the gate closed, the wind had started to whip down the lane, the rain came heavy again falling from what felt all directions the wind was squalling around, leaves and branches were being stripped from the trees lining the lane.

Thomas and Jervis set themselves at the back of the Yard there was cover under a wooden lean too, they sat on tree stumps amidst the storm overhead and started to eat and take some ale.

There was a banging at the gate, Jervis said will I ever get to eat? Thomas looked over the gate to see the ale seller and his cart, a flagon of ale for the Irenmonger, the dulcet tones of the ale man called across the gate, I will be said Jervis, the Ale seller reached to the back of his cart and lifted a flagon of ale, will you have one said Jervis to Thomas? I will he said, "is your beer cool?" asked Thomas, "It is" he replied, "I drew this ale this cool morning gentlemen, what say ye?" He asked, "we heard war is in the county" said Thomas, I too have heard that" said the Aleman," Richard the King is to move across these parts on his way to the roman roads to meet the Tudor "Tudor is that the name of the aggressor?" "it is said" replied the Aleman. "We will have to see said Jervis, we will keep out of the way of the King, he is welcome to pass by, but we do not wish for any engagement with his pressgangs." True and wise" said the Aleman, "I need my flagon back Smith and you Fletcher".

Jervis passed him two flagons and took two newly corked ones back over the fence. The Aleman said "Do you know Ruth Neville from Oddstone way?" " I do said Thomas , her father comes here for arrows and had his latch repaired, why?" "she passed away, the Lord took her early this morning following a heavy fever, her mother is besides herself with grief", "that is bad news" said Jervis, "my Son has a fever and is not well in his bed I hope it doesn't be that the lord is coming looking for all, the children seem to be hit hardest by this filthy French swett," " French?" said the Aleman? "Yes, the Bellman told us it was a French swett he told it had come without warning, It may have come with the French spies roaming about this area" Jervis continued, "Really?" said the Aleman, "Yes" said Thomas, "we have had a few in site of this very village!"

The rain started to fall again, the gentle pitter-patter turned to a torrent, the Aleman said "Thunderous shite, it's here again", "you may shelter here" said Jervis, "no thanking you gentlemen I will be on my way. It may only be a shower of gods tear, but it is most unwelcome.

The Aleman wrapped himself in an oilskin and him and his cart moved off up the village, shouting.

"Ale 'o Ale o'Ale for you. Good ale fine ale brings me your flagons ill fill them for you, and ales o ale o here is your beero".

CHAPTER 6

"So, brother let us talk again, what did you make of the priest words? what do you think he knows?" Asked Thomas, "It would seem that he does have some notice of impending troubles ahead", Jervis tore at his crust of bread with his teeth, he was looking directly into the embers of the fire , "perhaps he may of heard of this battle to come soon from the Civic Church in Leicester, we should use his advice and make sure the family is safe, I have a sword and a pike in my house," "I have the same" said Jervis, "we must use it to protect our loved ones", "yes indeed" replied Thomas.

The two brothers continued to sit in silence together, crunching a pear and eating some cheese curd, gulping the occasional drink of ale, wiping their mouths on the rough sackcloth shirt sleeves, they were both deep in thought, the only noise came from the rain pelting the roof of the lean too and some well-earned belches from the brothers against a backdrop of the splashing of the now heavy rain.

After a short while Thomas said, "I don't want to fight someone else's battle, I don't want to be away from the family," "I know brother" said Jervis, "we need to be here to protect not fighting away, I am not a coward or a shirker brother", Thomas looked across at Jervis, I have worked hard to get here, and I don't want to see me, you or the yard go for someone else's fight, either a King or a Duke."

You do understand?" Jervis nodded his head with a half-smile. Jervis stretched out his arm and slapped Thomas on the back "of course brother we are a family, and we need to stay that way". The brothers continued to drink and belch aloud, each belching getting louder as the Ale soaked the contents of their guts.

A few more minutes passed Thomas said, "and our work should be looked after or else we would not have a income". "Thomas please do not worry, we will get through whatever is coming, and with gods will and a blessing it might pass us by", Jervis tried to assure Thomas.

The two men sat there for a while, they heard horses coming down the lane, sloshing in the muddy filthy mire, four horses with soldiers mounted, the muffled horses hooves making a eerie sound as they passed, soon another four horses this time two riders and two horses loaded up with poles and tents, Thomas went to investigate Jervis pulled him down, "Stay out of sight" said Jervis, the rain was still falling heavily, the sound of it on the roof made it troublesome to hear , the two brothers sat in the shack in the yard as more soldiers moved past the yard.

A dozen four horses past the yard over a while, Jervis took a sneak look through the gate of the yard, he saw soldiers "definitely soldiers" he whispered to himself, some four men on horses, some two men and pack horses loaded, for what looked like for the setting of a camp.

Occasionally there was a lone soldier carrying a standard, wet and bedraggled the flag was that of Richard III. The cavalcade continued until early evening. There was something coming, and Jervis had a bad feeling in the pit of his stomach.

This Thursday evening, Thomas and Jervis and their wives would attend St Michaels Church and give thanks, there was much to do before the Church attendance and the weather was getting worse.

Thomas returned to his house, that evening the St Michael's church bell rang out calling villagers from Carltonstone and Barton to come together.

The address to the congregation was short, the priest making a reading to the 20 or so assembled there in the wet humid church, heeding the parishioners in their actions, a terrible battle was seen to be coming, These men passing through are on the way to the battle, the King, King Richard was coming from Leicester for a hard battle with Henry Tudor who was approaching the countryside locally from Roman road in Atherstone these may be new times for all of us, in this land far and wide. King Richard has bought with him 5000 men Leicester, there would be more men from Richard Knights and the Kings supporters from where they will set for battle somewhere nearby.

he also warned of the "Swett" or the "French

Swett's" telling the gathered that several people in the area had succumbed to the condition and suffered a quickness of death. "Beware of this tyrant of death" called the priest; "it hides itself amongst the poor and the wealthy and animal kind, it has no conscience it has no loyalty to man nor beasts open your windows and let gods' airs in your homes. "

He pleaded with the ladies of the congregation to cut and wear posies of wild mint sage and flavourful herbs to fight off the foul vapours talked about so much in recent days and weeks.

The priest then turned to the men of the village, be warned "there is conflict in the houses of York and Lancaster there is talk that a beleaguered King Richard is moving an army from Leicester City to defend his rights as King against an insurgent from overseas, warring army's may travel through this parish, do not succumb to the practice of Impressment, or drafting ways of the warlords."

"These soldiers and knights come for each other's death; they will not consider your soul in any man's battle. Do I make my words clear?" He looked around the church, Jervis and Thomas and several other men looked at each other, nods, and winks from men in the congregation were seen by the wives and the priest.

"That is all I can offer my sheep said the Priest, keep your families safe", Jervis raised his hand, the priest spotted him and gestured for him to stand and speak. "Yes, Jervis please speak to us."

Jervis stood and bowed to the Priest he clasped his leather cap in his hands. "We have over the last few days seen strange men in the woods at the back of the church, be warned these are not local men or men from Mercia, or Tamworth, these are French spies or so we were told, and it was suggested they could be, these men have their eyes on our village. "My boy is poorly in his bed; he may have caught the Frenchman's disease.

 The priest said "now, before you go casting doubt on these men how do you know they are spies?" Jervis continued "we had an officer from Leicester Assises staying with us one night, "he told me to be warned of French spies and that was what he said", ...".And!" said the priest "he also had a conversation with two such men with a hard spoken word and language not heard from round these parts, they swore obscenities at us in anger".

Another man in the church stood up and said "he had some foul birds stolen and had seen some men in the coppice woods under a tall tent cooking and drinking singing and shouting at each other."

A neighbour of Thomas stood up and said his wife had been troubled by three men in Redemoor market when she was selling her eggs and pears," they took from her several pears and filled their pockets full of eggs without payment or any thanks or favour, his wife was scared so she had not made a report to the toby of the marketplace. But they spoke strange words vicar".

"I see," said the priest. The weather was still very warm and seemed to be getting warmer, the sun was trying to break through the clouds swirling above.

The Priest took off his cap and replacing it after wiping his brow and neck. "Listen to me," he bellowed, "to all of you seated here today, I take your words and warnings, let us pray these troubled days to come pass us quickly and without distress or pain to your family's hearts, I repeat to you to take good care of your family. Stay far from trouble or conflict."

"Now good day to you all and God bless your homes and family", he waved his hands to gesture the end of the service and sermon, the congregation stood, and the vicar moved from the front of the church outside and stood at the door with the collection plate. Each woman and man passed by as he blessed them, Jervis got to the priest, "thank you Jervis" said the priest, "I know you will support those less fortunate, but do not go into battle for these Kings and conquerors I ask of you Jervis," Peter the priest took Jervis by the arm and held him tight, "I will not be," replied Jervis and "I expect my brother to not, as he is with me."

He said to Thomas "It is time to return home, secure your doors and family, I will call to you later at the back of the cottages, we will decide what to do with the family." "Agreed" said Thomas, they waited until the last four horses past then made secure the gate to the yard and made their way quickly across the mire that was now the lane, Jervis arrived home and called to Clara to come to him, Jervis said to Clara "close the shutters and secure the door, we must retire to the back of the cottage", "why? asked Clara "what is going on, what are those soldiers doing passing through the lane?"

"It is something that might be happening, but we don't know what", shouted Jervis, "where is your brother?" asked Clara, "he is safely with Anna and the children, we will have a talk together later, just make fast our home Clara, how is the boy?", "he is worse Jervis, burning up and delirious".

Jervis went up the small steps to the upper floor straight to his sons side, the 11 year old boy was on the bed, he was burning with fever and a cold sweat a small red face met Jervis in the dimness of light as he entered the tiny bedroom with its low roof line and crumbled ceilings.

"My Son are you unwell again?" "Yes, father" the boy coughed and sputtered his words, "do not move boy, I will get you a drink and some sage water", Jervis left the boys room and told Clara to "make some sage drink and a sage and water mint poultice for the boys' neck, wrap it up tightly in muslin and place it hard on the boys neck it will calm the heat in his skin."

"I will"" said Clara. Jervis made his way out of the back of the cottage to his brothers' cottage a few steps away, the rain was still falling. He called at the doorway, the rain was falling, and it was very wet underfoot and overhead. "Thomas, my boy is feverish and unwell, So, let us make this agreement, we will not be involved with the battle of other men, we must stay calm and stay close to Carltonstone".

Thomas said "we have our cousins in Smisby Jervis, we could walk there tomorrow by the Ashby trails, we could take the family there close the yard and wait till the conflict has moved away", jervis wiped the rain from his face "we have little chance or days to do that Thomas that is a bad journey many have been robbed at Measham and the boy is sick with swett so we should stay close at hand" said

Jervis, Thomas looked to the sky and the dark clouds and torrential rain falling," It is agreed brother, now go and tend to your boy. I hope he is well again soon."

Jervis returned in the rain he was now tired and cold, "come sit here by the fire" Clara insisted, "I have settled the boy he is sleeping now", "that is good said Jervis, "yesterday when we were at the market the Bellman spoke of the swett, a disease which has killed many folk and quickly, I hope he has not caught bad favour with the French swett, these men in the area may have bought foul airs with them and our boy caught an ill breath from it?" "I don't know what and why you talk of this Jervis!" said Clara "we must pray for him and hope the poultice works".

The two sat almost in silence their young boy on their minds, Jervis drank the last of the ale, Clara took time sewing a cap then said, "come Jervis it is evening, let us have an early rest and go to our bed". "Yes, I am tired and weary let us close the doors and see tomorrow". Jervis didn't take any persuading and lead the way.

The two made their way to the bed, calling in on the boy, he was sleeping well although his breathing was shallow, Jervis turned him onto his side and re soaked the poultice, replacing it on the boy's neck. Clara covered the boy and left his shutter ajar to let fresh air into the room.

As Jervis lay in the bed, he heard more carts and horses pass his cottage, he thought there could be an army on the move.

Jervis rested but slept lightly waking often, he took a candle to the boy who was delirious in the night and calling out, Jervis cooled his fever with a cloth dipped in water then rung out wiped across his brow and chest. The boy settled and stopped calling, Clara came to the boy's bedside and took over from Jervis, "you go back to sleep" she smiled, "I will look after him", she lay her hand on top of his, he smiled and said, "it will be a good outcome". She said, "I know I believe it."

Jervis returned to bed he slept till dawn, then rose and went to see where Clara was, she was sleeping her head on her son's bedside her hand in his, she was sleeping the boy was still, he was cool, Jervis looked twice, he called out "Clara"! she woke immediately and with a start, "oh lord" she called, he shook the boy, he didn't move, Jervis stepped in and shook him and called out "John"! Jervis's heart was beating in his head ignoring the mornings silence for those few moments.

CHAPTER 7

The boy lay there, he moaned and called out for his mother. "Oh lord oh lord" called Jervis, the boy smiled and asked for food and a drink, the fever was over, and he was cooler, Jervis flung opened the shutters and the cool air of the dawn freshened the room.

Jervis went to the door of his cottage where he could hear someone tapping on the door, when he opened the door Thomas was standing there, "Morning to you Thomas", Thomas said "look brother yonder" Thomas was pointing across the field, the mist was low and still, Jervis could see three men standing on the opposite side of the river, they were all looking back to Carltonstone, "who are they Jervis? I don't know but they look like the visitors you had yesterday, one of them is a bowman. Come let us go to the yard and prepare, I think we are in for another visit from strangers."

The brothers returned to their homes, they secured the doors and told their wives not to venture out, they crossed the lane to open the yard. Jervis got to work on the fire in the forge hearth, Thomas was scrambling over the wood pile getting some long staves from the wood store at the rear of the yard.

Jervis turned and under the bench he retrieved two halberd heads, rusted, and deformed, he set to work hammering them to a fine finish, ensuring the balance and trial fitting them to each of the truest oak staves, Thomas has whittled the oak staves they were now true and strong, they had been two years in the making, so had weathered and were light in the feel.

Thomas went back to the cottage and bought back a collection of Arrows and sat fitting bodkins he melted pitch and fitted each one, he checked the fletching before putting them headfirst in a bucket of water, letting the pitch set and the wooden shaft of the arrow to swell holding the bodkin firm and solid.

The halberds were broken they had a slim blade and a rounded poke, it was an old Scottish design he had swapped for a moor's sword and scabbard, in the market.

Jervis had been working on them from time to time, he never thought the day may come where he would be needing them. It took a whole day of hard toil, heat and skilful fashioning of the dim rusting metals, Jervis had finished the halberd with a quenching of the red-hot blade and its ball ended poke in tallows and rancid oils blueing them down. He spent time burnishing the blade and poke with an ironstone. After the two brothers finished their weapons, Jervis was satisfied they had something to protect themselves, should the worse happen.

Throughout the day, still more archers strode through the village their feet and leggings dark with the mud and filth made by the wet rain and flooded lanes of recent days, singing as they went by, as they left the village, they marched southeast of Redemoor, as far as Thomas could see the lanes were full, shoulder to shoulder of archers, pikemen and soldiers making their way towards the hill to the south of the Redemoor vale.

Thomas said, "the day is darkening; these men are still coming Jervis what is going to happen". "Let us not consider our darkest worries Thomas" Jervis was concerned, and his worry was clear to see in his eyes, he said "we must eat and make secure our home's Thomas, this is a bad time ahead of us we must not show ourselves for a fear of being impressed into battle against our will or for that, our understanding.

Into the yard rushed William Barker from the top of Green Lane, "Jervis! - Jervis!" "Yes William, I hear you", "Jervis hear me, there are men marching into the lanes many of them, all carrying weapons of war", Yes William we know we have seen them too", William was stuttering his words, "I,I have heard they are making their way in the sight of the roman road at Merevale", Jervis tried to calm William, "that may be true William, but we don't know why"? "It is a war Jervis; this is the war of York against the Lancastrians the war of the roses as we have come to know it and now it is with us".

William , William, Jervis tried to slow his garbled words down, William stood there wringing his hands and stuttering " It is upon us now Jervis what should we do"? Jervis responded in a stern voice, "Go home lock the doors and let them pass by they bear you no harm", it was clear William was in a state of panic, "do not worry your family about this" Jervis advised William, "go home and let it pass, if there is a battle then it will be far off in another county".

No! Jervis Listen to me! William interrupted; "the other armies are travelling to this neighbourhood from Tamworth". "That may be more serious than we would have prayed for, there seems to be a battle ahead somewhere close by".

"Thomas!", Jervis called his brother over and spoke softly but directly, "go to your home and make it secure" then we will meet again in the back of the cottages", "I will said Thomas", "I ask you William return to your family , spread these words if you see any others in the lane," "I will" said William, he ran off up the hill in the village to his own home. Jervis had heard previously of homes being burnt out in a rout from a battle, he was sure it was to embellish the story, but his father used to tell him of conflicts where the losing soldiers would take terrible revenge on a local settlement.

Jervis looked beyond the tops of the gates in his yard, he could see the top of the lane and the road into Redemoor, it was thick with soldiers' marching shoulder to shoulder, column by column, all carrying weapons of war, some trailing small canons and slings, horses by the dozens and mounted with armoured and leather aproned soldiers.

The stench was horrible, a mixture of sweat, horse shit and filth filled the air, it was a stifling smell made worse in the warm August afternoons muggy air, some soldiers were singing hymns as they marched and rode their skinny horses up to Redemoor, some marched in a sombre silence carrying the standard of the King to a steady drumbeat.

It was clear to Jervis this was not a skirmish as he had witnessed several times before, this was not a local fight or disagreement between landowners, this was something far more serious, something he saw as a real battle of war, the war of the roses had arrived on his doorstep, he felt anxious, he felt worried for his family, his son, his brother and his wife and his own wife, in a matter of an afternoon the scene in Jervis's world had become dark, very dark and foreboding.

Jervis made his way into his home, the wasps were still in the cottage, he opened the shutters to the rear of the cottage and with a wetted rag wafted the wasps out of the lower room, he placed some green tree branches onto the hearth, they slowly flamed up and filled the room with a thick white grey smoke, he continued to wave the wasps out of the shutter openings clearing most of them away.

Clara appeared, she said "what is happening Jervis why are all these men here", "there is a battle going to happen and soon I think Clara" Jervis was doing his best to stay calm, "I want you and the boy to remain here in the home, do not venture out without my say so. It will not be safe to do so for a few days". Jervis was still waving the last few wasps from the room, "So, I will fetch water and make some provisions for this end of this week" "Oh Jervis" Clara cried, what will happen to us?" "Be quiet woman!" Jervis shouted at Clara we will be fine Clara! stop please"!

Thomas came to the rear of the cottage, "Jervis do you want me to seal the well?".

"Not before we have taken water for our drinking" Jervis held a pale up , Thomas took it " but later we must put the large stone on the top" Jervis said.

"I will need your help" "of course" said Thomas. The two men drew water from the well, the four pales were filled, this was one of four wells in the village, the recent rainfall had muddied the water a little, but it would settle out in time.

Thomas placed the large wheel top on the well and both men lifted the huge square stone of granite and placed it on the top. Thomas thought it was wise to close the well in case the rats and filth from the road would find its way into the water, Jervis knew the lid being sealed was for another reason. He didn't trouble his younger brother with his concerns. Jervis took a walk up the village lane and advised the other well keepers to close their wells too.

He arrived back to his home, the gates of the forge were closed and secured, it was quieter, he entered his home to be greeted by Clara, she said" vicar Peter called could he go to the chapel right now?" "Yes, of course I will go shortly" Jervis took Clara's arm and reassured her things would be resolved in time, Clara said "I was worried about the boy", Jervis said "It will be what it will be this is not our scrap, we must be safe, and we will be", he made his way to the door.

The rain had started to fall again, he took a cloak and made his way to the Church a few yards down the main street.

There the priest was waiting for him, "Jervis, oh Jervis thank you for coming, this is a terrible thing happening all around us I will be calling the congregation to be here this evening", "That will be a good thing Peter" said Jervis "you can put peoples mind at ease", "it does look as if we are being invaded". Peter said, "The villagers listen to you Jervis, can I ask that you make a few words to them they will appreciate the words coming from a local man as well as the lord's words from me". "Yes, I will, if it will help" said Jervis, "ring the chapel bell when you are ready".

When Jervis went outside the rain was torrential again the lane was a river of water and mud. Jervis made his way back to his home, Clara and the boy were waiting for him, "Father, Father called the boy what is going on I can hear drums beating and strange men in the village bowmen and archers are here", "please don't worry my son, this is a fight of the King" Jervis tired again to reassure Clara and the boy.

"He will be close by in the next days or so, we must pray the battle is short and the King returns a victory against the aggressor", "who is the aggressor Jervis"? asked Clara, "we don't really know, the stories are confused, but I have heard there is a challenger to the throne, and he is called Henry Tudar", Jervis sipped from his goblet, the continued, "I am unsure if it is that of his army that is marching this way".

"If it is, well then Clara", Jervis stopped speaking and thought a little and then said, "may the lord have mercy on all our souls. this could be a bloody battle".

CHAPTER 8

There was banging on the door of the cottage, it was Seth from the toll house, "come quickly he said there is a cart with a broken wheel on the Barton Lane, it is imperative it is repaired, come quickly", "Why? said Thomas "it can wait until tomorrow, tell the cart driver to bring it back tomorrow there are more pressing things in our hands right now," Seth held his hat in his hands, "Thomas, Jervis you don't understand the King is here, it is his cart in the royal cortege !",Seth stood there in silence "I mean really you must come now! please Jervis", The two brothers looked at each other and looked at Seth who was clearly troubled by this.

Thomas and Jervis set off it was a half mile walk, the rain was incessant still, they came across a cart a four-wheeler, the front of the cart was in a ditch, one of the back wheels was off the ground and it load had been partly shed when it fell into the ditch, "it has been raining so hard said the driver, I couldn't see my way". Behind it were more carts all carrying provisions, further back a much more important set of carriages were lying in wait.

Thomas said "we must pull the cart from the ditch I cannot repair it there", six burley men appeared, they cleared the sacks and boxes from the back of the cart, and then, all took a grip of the wheels and pulled they slipped in the deep mud and mire near to the wooden bridge they managed to pull it slowly free of the gully, the wheel had lost a spoke and it had buckled the wheel. Thomas said you "will not be able to steer this cart with this wheel broken I will need to repair it in my yard."

"No!" said one of the bigger men, he was dressed

in a leather jerkin and shoulder pads of heavy leather, he had a chainmail cover jacket he was obviously a military man, "you go and get what you need, and I will make sure the King knows", he growled, "King"? said Jervis, "You heard me villain now get this wheel repaired and quickly" the big man growled his instructions. Jervis said to Thomas "go and get some spokes we will fashion a new one here, these men can lift the cart with my help you take Seth with you and come back quickly".

Thomas and Seth ran off in the direction of Carltonstone, Jervis appealed to the soldiers to get a branch from a fallen tree not far from the side of the road Jervis rolled a log out from the lane side and they levered the cart into the air raising the damaged wheel, Jervis took a look, "this is not favourable" he said to the soldier, "it matters not! it must be put right into service and we must move shortly"

"I will remove the wheel", said Jervis, "I will need your men's help to raise the wheel again Sir". Jervis found an axe on the back of the cart, he used the hammer end to hammer out the cotter from the hub of the wheel, it was not a good cotter and was made of a soft wood.

A short while later Thomas arrived with an armful of tools and odd spokes, the two men set to work, they managed to remove the end of the broken spoke and offer a replacement to the wheel with a chisel and the axe, Thomas fashioned a spoke end, he removed the felloes and with oak pins and a new cotter had made the repaired spoked wheel roll true.

As Thomas was working to get the cotter to fit the hub, the soldier said you work together well, "we are brothers" replied Jervis, "I am the blacksmith and my brother there is a wheelwright, it is well that you found us so close by". The Soldier shook Jervis by the hand "It is truly fortunate, we are in convoy and behind us villager, he lowered his voice and whispered "is the King, his progress must not be Impeded as we are called to battle" "We had noticed something coming to the area, where are you heading? asked Jervis, "We are due to be an Anne Beame Hill near a place called Shenton by night fall or before then, our camp is in waiting", "I see said Jervis, may God be with you", "and with you smith" said the soldier, the Soldier walked away and turned he asked Jervis, "how far is it to Anne Beame Hill from here "? Jervis responded, "it is only 4 or 5 long miles Sir," "very good, I will pass the message back myself."

He walked back along the cavalcade to a covered carriage , he stood back and addressed the occupants, after several exchanges the canvas was curled back and a man got out of the carriage, he was short and was shouting and pointing at the soldier, he walked towards Jervis and Thomas as they worked, the sweat on Thomas brow was clear to see, it was dripping from his nose as he struggled to get the cotter to seat into the hub, Jervis too was working hard to right the large four wheeler and get the wheel to roll freely.

"Men! Shouted the short man, can you expedite yourselves this convoy needs to move and move now"!, Thomas called back "it is almost ready Sire" without looking up his eyes locking with Jervis.

Jervis removed his cap and addressed the short man, "the cart is now ready Sire, you have not far to go , so it will be serviceable for your needs", "about time"! was the reply , he turned on his heels and walked off toward the back of the convoy, all around soldiers were loading the cart up again, the short man had a limp and a strange gate, Jervis noticed his stature, he turned and said to the taller soldier who seemed to be in charge, "and Sir may I ask who will pay us for our work here sir, "Pay? Pay?" said the soldier his foul breath turning Jervis's stomach "it is to keep the King in safe hands that is payment enough Sir".

He bellowed at Jervis almost nose to nose, Jervis remained silent as he held his breath and through this Thomas looked on, Jervis didn't budge "be on your way or ill slit your cheeky neck"! The soldier quipped. Thomas stepped forward, Jervis held him back with his hand, "not now" said Jervis, the tall soldier returned to his horse, Seth was instructed to help the solider mount his horse, he held his hands out to cut the Soldiers foot with a grunt and a lift he mounted it and gestured for the convoy to move forward.

Jervis Thomas and Seth stood to one side as the cart pulled away, the foot soldiers walked close behind, as the convoy moved forward.

The covered cart with the short man in it came level with the three men, Jervis looked up as the canvas was pulled back, the short man was looking directly at Jervis and Thomas, he slowly nodded his head, Jervis bowed his head in return, Nothing was said, Thomas said to Jervis "why do you bow your head to a crippled debtor Jervis?, "I suspect the only reason I can give you Thomas is to save our necks!"

Thomas, Seth, and Jervis picked up the tools and other wheel parts, they walked slowly along Barton Lane the light was starting to fade, Thomas continued to complain to Seth of no payment. As they got to the toll house the convoy was moving and started to thin out, to mostly men on horseback. Seth went ahead into the toll house and came out carrying a flagon, "here Jervis and Thomas this is an offering, it was my doing, asking you to attend to that cart, I am sorry you were not rewarded, they could have pushed it off the lane, however you rescued them," Thomas said "Thanks to you Seth that is a kind thought, will you come a join us one evening for tales and a drink,? im sure Peter and Thomas will join us". "I would like that" said Seth, well in that case will put this aside for such an evening"".

"Good evening Jervis and good evening to you Thomas", Thomas didn't answer and continued down the man lane into Carltonstone.

As they approached the cottages and the yard, Jervis called to Thomas who was still mumbling, "Thomas! Stop your whining boy, we did a good deed today with the broken wheel", "how do you work that one" said Thomas still disgruntled at not being paid, "that short man," yes! with the limp yes! what of the ignorant feckless fickle" said Thomas, "well that was the King, this convoy was his cavalcade."

"You talk such tripe sometimes Jervis" Thomas said as he elbowed the gate to the yard ajar. Then Thomas stopped placed his tools on the work bench and looked at Jervis, "yes" said Jervis "has the groat dropped? "The King?" Thomas said, "the real King?"

"Yes," said Jervis, "I am sure of his description, his convoy must be weaving through the lanes to prevent an ambush. Did you not see the flags and standards"? Thomas was deep in thought, "That could mean the aggressor may be close by or here amongst the villages and hamlets now, it might give reason to why those men were in the market midweek and why there have been men across the river, they could not be the Kings men, but as the bellman said spies are amongst this place."

"But they are not here now" Jervis said, "look, yes, I know they have fled on seeing the convoys, bowmen and soldiers moving through the lanes. I would be surest of that too".

Thomas asked what was in the flagon from Seth? "Mead wine said Jervis, he always makes mead wine and his is a good tonic for many ills including a bad story which he can make."

Just then the bell of the small Church rang, Clara came to the door, "why is the bell ringing? Clara asked, "I know not why wife, I will go and see", said Jervis. Peter was at the door of the Church waving to Jervis. Jervis could see someone else just inside the entrance. Several other men were coming to see why the bell was being rang.

Jervis looked back and called to Thomas; "come

Thomas this is for all of us". Jervis made his way into the church yard a small garden filled with yew, cherry and pretty wildflowers nestled besides the many wooden crosses and freshly mounded graves.

As Jervis entered the church, he was greeted by Richard Sharnford the Kings witness. "Hello to you again" said Jervis looking a little confused, "Reverend Peter what is all this about on a hot warm Friday evening?" Jervis enquired.

"Please sit-down men of Carltonstone. I have instructions and news for you". Clearly Reverend Peter was troubled, and his face was ashen and his eyes wide with concerns.

"This is Richard of Sharnford, he has just ridden from Atherstone where he has been on the Kings business, he has asked to address you all, he is indebted to Jervis Smith and wanted to give you news and advice".

"We are obliged" said Jervis,

"Please listen and take heed of his words".

He held out his palm toward Richard Sharnford. Richard took to his feet and called out "Villagers of Carltonstone, as you may know there has been much activity in the area overnight and today, there is set a battle between our King, King Richard and between a nobleman called Henry Tudar, the whereabouts of both challengers is not known but will be clear in the coming short time".

This evening Anne Beame hill a two mile walk from here, this is the camp for the King, the lord holy King Richard III, is not known to be there yet he is making his way from Bow Bridge in the city of Leicester", Jervis looked across the room at Thomas, Thomas raised his eyebrows, if what they had seen earlier was true, then The King was already there.

Richard Sharnford continued " his command under the Duke of Norfolk has taken a firm vantage point and it is suspected his camp will offer the best view of the vale of Fenn lanes, Dadlyngton and Shenton, he is enforced by the Duke of Northumberland and the Duke of Norfolk , so more armies are fighting on the side of King Richard III, it is hoped and prayers are being said that this will be a short battle and the aggressor Tudar is sent running from this place."

Sharnford cleared his throat, "Be under no doubts in your mind, that this is a dangerous and serious situation in your parishes, I will advise to all men not to be drawn into a fight with any stranger to your knowing, these are mercenary man of great battle experience and to despatch a man from this earth is their daily business and it is their duty, Sharnford looked down and shuffled his mud encrusted boots then looked directly at Jervis "your life at their hands shares the same valuate as a common rabbit, the snapping of your neck or drawing your guts with a shit covered hand knife is of little challenge for them and they will do it in the name of the Lord."

Sharnford cast his gaze around the room at the other villagers, "I urge you to stay away, he stopped for a while to catch his breath "keep your women and children locked out of sight, pillaging isn't unheard of in battles and local fighting, it is feared this is far more serious and requires of you for the best of caution".

Reverend Peter stepped forward to the small gathering of 13 men, "do you hear that advice men of Carltonstone? stay away from this fighting it will be dreadful and full of injury and painful deaths, you need to have no part in it to be loyal to the crown, so my advice is that of the lord to desist the urge to attend to see the spectacle."

Sharnford stood forward his stature and broad shoulders almost filling the room he spoke quietly "A similar advice is being sent to all the other villages surrounding Redemoor."

Thomas stood forward, "what do we do if we need to defend our homes?" a man called out from the back, Richard Sharnford looked around all the men and said "fight with all your might, but I do say to you again, these men are men of war, they are strong well organised in the dealings of death and will if given the chance dispatch you off to the lord and only then ask a question after your demise".

He took a deep breath, "do not risk your families' lives stay hidden away. If you can go north of the mighty river Trent for a few days, then do so! My advice is firm to you all stay away from this fight or the fight will come to you."

The men gathered' muttered amongst themselves, Jervis spoke up "it is understood, and I hope so ,Reverend Peter and Richard, my thanks to you for your advice, Jervis turned to Richard and asked of him" how will you see out the battle? you are an official are you not sir", "I am an Alderman" said Richard Sharnford, "I will be an observer and Kings Witness, I will make my way to Anne Beame Hill this night".

"I will not fight unless I am approached by the enemy and will otherwise defend myself and that of my office."

Jervis shook his hands then Peters hands and stepped out into the darkness he and Thomas made their way back to their homes, "Jervis!" someone called his name from behind, it was

Richard Sharnford, "I ask another favour from you Jervis", "yes what is it?" replied Jervis, "Do you have a gentlemen's knife I can buy from you?"

A gentleman's knife was longer than a dagger but shorter than a short sword.

Jervis answered immediately, "No Richard Sharnford I do not! then he said, "but I do have one I can loan to you on the promise that in good time you return it and, on the hope, my friend, that you do not have to use it".

"Again, Jervis, you have me in your debt and disadvantage, I am appreciative of your thoughtful regards."

"However,", Richard continued, I must insist that you hold my monies until I return with your knife, do we have an agreement"? Richard held out his hand to make a deal, "we do" said Jervis" "Give me your cap, I will place the 20 groats in here and you can pick it up on your return".

Jervis went into a box held secure with ropes and a large stone near the back of the yard, from it he produced a Gentleman's knife, new with a leather-bound hilt and in a leather scabbard "this one is sharp enough to shave your beard" said Jervis as he handed it to Richard.

"This is a fine knife", said Richard "well balanced" he commented as he moved it back and forth.

The glow of the forge made it easier to see the detail on the broad bladed knife. "Thank you, Jervis,", responded Richard, "I must make my way", "bring it back to me safely with yourself alive Richard, make use of your own words and may god bless you", "good evening to you too", said Richard as he mounted his horse and trotted up the filthy and muddy track leading out of the village and up to Redemoor along the Barton Lane.

CHAPTER 9

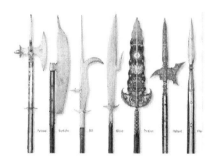

The two brothers returned to their cottages, they were both dirty and hungry, Anna was pleased to see Thomas and the children came to be with him too. Anna offered Thomas some food and a drink of ale he said he "would need to wash the day away" , she had a new shirt set aside for his return, he washed at the side of the well and scrubbed his hands and face, he noticed splinters in the palms of his hands, he pulled at them to release them as he did they bled and for a few seconds he watched as his blood trailed down past his thumbs and onto this wrists dripping into the pale below.

It made him think of his life and wife and children, it made him angry that on this day someone else's fight was being carried out on his own doorstep and putting at risk his life and that of his family.

He washed away the blood and cleaned down the pale and washing area. He watched as spiders and wood lice scurried away, he wished that was the fate of the soldiers he had seen today.

Thomas sat down with Anna and the children and ate his meal of stew and bread; he ate fruit berries and pears and drank his ale. His mind was elsewhere and distracted from Anna and her recollection of the day with the children in the fields adjacent.

What is it Thomas asked Anna, "Oh nothing my wife Anna", he was thoughtful for a moment or two then said "I've seen the King today and it has made me realise how dangerous these battles are, I have always heard of them but until today thought they were far away battles, but today has made me think", "think about what?"

asked Anna, he focused on Anna held out his and touched hers, "oh you my love, our children and our new arrival".

"Where did you see the King? She asked, "On Barton Lane, skulking into the area by the back door, we mended and made good his broken wheel, we had no reward for our good deeds so some King to me Anna a debtor now in my eyes, I hope he survives this battle and has the appreciation of my work to come and pay his way".

"What did he look like?" asked Anna, Thomas gave her an account of what he had seen of the short bow-legged limping person, and said "if it wasn't for Jervis knowing who it was, I would have dismissed him there and then?"

Anna said, "there was a man came this evening, he left this bag and told me to give this to Thomas the wheelwright", she went to the mantle shelf and on it was a brown leather pouch, she took it down and handed it to Thomas, he said "when was this?"

"This evening when you were at the church, he came to the door and said give this to the wheelwright that's all", Anna Smiled and gave Thomas the little bag, "so what is it? "Thomas Took the bag from Anna, He was intrigued, Thomas placed his hand inside and pulled out 20 Groats all new coins," well im blessed" said

Thomas "look at this, this must be for the wheel we remade today".

"I must tell Jervis "He said excitedly, He walked the few feet to Jervis's home, Jervis came to the door and said with a big smile on his face "ah Thomas guess what?"

"I don't know what brother, know What?!" said Thomas, "look" Jervis held out his hand, in Jervis's hand was 20 groats, Thomas was laughing and showed Jervis his wages, look brother I have the same, the King did pay his debt to us after all".

"We should thank him by going to watch him beat his aggressor, shall we go at dawn in the morning? Thomas said, "we were warned brother not to peruse the battle", Jervis said, Thomas seemed to be excited by the prospect "we could go and watch from Dadlyngton brother it is higher than Ann Beame Hill it would offer a safe vantage from there"? "No Thomas we are responsible for the comfort of our family, we must stay here, that is my final word".

"We have work to do, you have Henry Congers new wheels to lay out," "I know Jervis" said Thomas, "but I've never seen a battle and it would be good spirit to support the King now he has rewarded us for our toil today". "This is foolish talk brother stop it now, I'll hear no more from you" Jervis scolded Thomas and pushed Thomas back out and closed the door, Thomas returned to Anna and the children.

The two brothers had closed the yard and made secure their doors and settled in for the night.

Some long miles away the troops for the King Richard III were assembling their canons and bringing food and ale to the soldiers in the camp, there were a lot of march hungry men to feed and prepare for the next morning regardless of what was to be expected.

Richard was firm in his ambition to make the first strike against Tudur, messengers were back and forth to a central line at White moor with messages from the dukes of Northumberland and the duke of Norfolk.

Both sides exchanges insults and challenges to each other throughout the build-up.

Thomas rose early before dawn, his mind restless was on the war due to start at any time, he was desperate in his mind to want to see what happens and made his way to get dressed he put on a long coat of leather and wool, he made his way to the yard and went inside to retrieve is bow and a fist full of arrows and his dagger. He strapped his bow to his shoulder and turned to set off, there in his face was Jervis.

"And where do you think you are going brother?" Jervis insisted and answer, Thomas said "im going to view the battle Jervis, I want to see the war, I don't want to fight and will not fight."

"Remember what Richard Sharnford said brother they are men of war they are paid to kill; their business is your death. Why risk it?" Thomas face looked beaten by reason, but not enough to quell his determination, "Something tells me I must" Thomas replied.

Jervis looked to the ground; he scratched his chin.

"The only way you will be going to see this is if I come with you. We can look out for each other my young brother." Thomas 's eyes opened wide and a broad smile came across his face.

Jervis returned to his home and woke Clara; "I am going out and will be back late morning or in the afternoon. Please don't go" she asked of him, "I must Clara, but we will be safe together", "please come back to me" she pleaded. "I will Clara, don't worry, I will be cautious." He left and Clara sobbed in her pillow.

It was still dusky and dark overhead, a bright

moon was low on the horizon lighting the way, they walked in silence together side by side, as the brothers made their way across the lanes towards Anne Beame hill on the other side of Redemoor, a journey on foot of lanes and fields woods and coppice, they arrived as dawn was just breaking, the orange and yellow sun breaking through the low clouds, its dappled and broken shepherds warning beams of light shining through to the day over and between the hills as they rose brilliantly on the Shenton end of the Anne Beame hill.

There were in immediate sight 100's of soldiers, a whole garrison had appeared overnight and from the previous day.

The smoke from fires curled up slowly in the still dawn air. Thomas and Jervis stayed far away and down out of sight. They were in a wood near to the hollows at the back of the hamlet.

It was in tha' the Morn and then after King Richard, furnished thoroughly with all manner of things, drew his whole host out of their tents, and arrayed his battleline, stretching it forth of a wonderful length, so full replenished both with footmen and horsemen that to the beholders afar off it gave a terror for the multitude, and in the front were placed his archers, like a most strong trench tha' bulwark;

of these archers he made leader John Duke of
Norfolk. After this long battleline followed the
King himself, with a choice force of soldiers

CHAPTER 10

And I my selfie will hover on
this Anne Beame hill
That ffaire battle ff'r to see.
Sir William, wise and wealthy,
Was hindmost at the outsetting.
Men said that day that did him see,
He came betime unto our King (Henri)

After a while Thomas was eager to see more and wanted to get closer, Jervis said "no it was too risky, they still could be arrested and held as spies even executed without trial".

Thomas pointed out 2 huge Oak trees to their right, slightly higher than the surrounding wood lands, let us climb high said Thomas there is plenty of leaf cover and we will remain out of sight.

Thomas and Jervis shinned up the first bow of the tree then climbed further, as they did they could see over the hump and in to the bowl shape of the vale from the top of Anne Beame hill, what was before them was a sight of amazement and wonder there were many men 10's of 100's row after row of colourful battle lines, swathed in an early morning mist hanging low on the flat Fenn fields each line was flanked by more men all marked in neat ranks with King Richard III standards flying high.

In the distance Thomas could see another army far way on the flats of Fenn laynes, that looked as if it was a much bigger garrison and it stretch back many acres to where the river met the old roman road, there were ranks and ranks of men, some on horseback, some on foot, many halberds and helmets shone in the early beam of the sun now coming over the hill at the rear of Ann Beame hill as the light was getting better ist was becoming more apparent how many soldiers would be fighting in battle.

Thomas was aware of his nerves; he knew he shouldn't have come but he just wanted to see what this amassing of huge numbers of men was about. What was before him was a wonderment no villager or villain would ever have seen. The immense organisation, the volume of men, uniforms, horse's, food kitchens weapons bowmen, buckets, and buckets of arrows all with hardened bodkin made for piercing the best of armour were set in waiting.

The smell about in the heat was an eye watering a gut-wrenching stench of horse shit and filth from 1000's of soldiers pissing in the rivers and wood land.

Flies were amassing a swarm of saw flies biting, leaving a sore itchy wound, it wouldn't be a good time to join in the mire below. Jervis thought of the effect of a hot day on the horses would bring, water pale after pale, was being carried from the river to the horse's,

After a short while his inquisitive mind was satisfied, he whispered across to Jervis, "let us go now I've seen enough". Jervis put his fingers to his mouth to stop Thomas talking and to be quiet, he pointed below.

There in the lane below literally feet from the trees they were perched in, was a pair of soldiers, on horseback. They were talking and discussing food they were busy chatting in bawdy detail of the busty wench, who served them sustenance and comfort at the Blue Boar Inn.

Jervis was scared and was gesturing to Thomas that they were not to be messed with, Jervis whispered back "not now let us wait until they have gone".

The two soldiers were guarding the entrance to the lane leading up to Anne Beame woods and the hill. Thomas has slid out along a bow high up in the canopy, Jervis was in the tree next to it high on a branch sitting comfortably.

The breeze was starting to get up as the dawn sun moved the air up from the ground, it wasn't strong it was very gentle; Thomas was enjoying the gentle sway of the tree as it made for a good view through the leaves and a relaxing early morning. It was cool but Jervis was sure it would be another hot day, perhaps with more rain later which for being in a tree in heavy rain isn't a good place to be.

The two soldiers were talking below and to each other extolling the virtues of a lady they both knew, each recalled a wench at the blue boar, she wore the best under attire, had the roundest biggest breasts was the prettier and cooked the best wild boar and cakes, she was equally the best ale wench in the Leicester county and they both had love for her, each soldier has serviced the wench in so many different ways and places, each one trying to outdo the other, sadly to Jervis it sounded like they were both in love with the same wench.

He chuckled to himself letting out a little laugh, the soldiers stopped in their tracks and mid-sentence and looked around their halberds set ready they listened.

"Fox!" one said "a soon to be dead fox" said the other. One of the soldiers slapped the other on the back and said "let us despatch some ignorant Frenchmen". "No my friend, let us eat first", they dismounted from their horses and on foot marched off together, only to be replaced by two more bigger broader men taking up the guarding of the lane.

They lent their poleaxes next to the tree where the brothers were hiding, they were eating a half-chewed leg of mutton, some baked apples, and onions every now and then they took turns in swigging on a flagon of ale, they stood there silent munching spitting the gristle out wandering up and down the lane.

At a certain time, the drummers started to beat their drums there were 30 or so drummers stood on top of the hill, they drummed out a regular beat, this was followed by the trumpeters making the battle call, then back to the drummers, like a heartbeat it drummed out. In the distance Thomas heard the drum beat from the other army on the flats, it was louder as there were 100 or more drummers.

They made out a beat too like a regular slow heartbeat. Pacing time, marking the time, but making sure they didn't beat in time with the drummers on Anne Beame hill, dum, dum, dum, dum, dum, again the trumpeters sounded out the fanfare of war, then back to the drum, dum, dum, dum, dum, dum, it was almost a sombre, dark, unnerving, miserable noise heralding certain death, each side made the same gesture, this went on for a long time. the sight was incredible the colours of each resplendent in the low morning sunlight.

From their vantage point high in the trees the brothers could see all but a small part of the battlefield on the eastern side. As jervis looked down the far side of Anne Beame Lane he could see Richard Sharnford he was entering one of the bigger camp tents, he re appeared later carrying a halberd and mounted his horse riding down the hill towards Jervis and Thomas, look whispered Thomas "there is

Richard Sharnford what is he doing?"

"I don't know"! replied to Jervis from a whisper, Sharnford, cantered along the lane passing just under the two brothers hidden high in the tree-tops. He stopped and spoke to the large soldiers below. They moved away, Sharnford, literally, a few yards from the tree the brothers were in stopped his horse.

As he stopped there, he placed his halberd in a sling on the side of the horse.

He then called in a loud voice, without looking up,

"I can see you two brothers from Carltonstone, I see you hiding in those trees, you promised me that you would not come to see this, Please I ask of you go home now whilst you can". He waited for a reply, he took a big breath in exasperation.

"Jervis, Thomas!, come on!", Richard continued with a louder voice, "believe me there will be a chaos here very shortly" Jervis said "how did you know I was here? "Richard replied "I called on your home this morning to see you, Clara your wife said you had come to look at the battle, she was very tearful Jervis, so for her sake your son and Thomas' children's sake go home."

 "If you are discovered, you will be enlisted to fight to the death today, this morning! Think on that you two, you are not Soldiers, you are not warriors, you are good people, let the soldiers heralded here today do your fighting for you."

"Think on this, there will be no appeals, or prayers said for your poor souls, your dead corpses will rot in those fields, you will be mutilated, cut down and nameless, you are here to witness death, and there will be the holy lord's amount, Go Home! Your family awaits your safe return."

"We will go as soon as you go" called down Jervis, "you have our word", at that point an almighty boom sounded out across the field loud cheering came from the other army, a plume of white smoke drifted across the vale, it was the first cannon shot one let off to find its range, a few moments later boom! another volley of two cannon were fired. Finding their landing short of the ranks across the fields.

The cry went out " Yeaaaaagh"! And the rattling of swords and poleaxes sounded out from one set of ranks across the vale to the other, each time the cannon sounded off the battle cry and insults were flying.

The drumming continued dum dum dum dum dum dum. Then another fanfare. "My friends" Sharnford called out "it is really time for you to return home".

"We will" said Jervis "we will". "Good said Sharnford, "do not doubt my words, I will meet you in a couple of days I owe you my debt".

At that Richard Sharnford galloped off down the lane towards the opposition on the far side of the vale. There he was met by someone from across the vale they exchanged words and Sharnford made his was back breaking through a fence and on up to the top of the hill.

On the top of the hill was the short man, they had seen on the previous afternoon and evening, he was short in stature and his back was bent over, he was wearing a fine shirt and ruffle, his cape was edged with a gold thread and embroidery, stout boots and a solid leather belt, his limp seemed more pronounced as he was wearing leg armour and was still being fitted with gauntlets and a breast plate.

There was a glorious stallion horse standing by with fine saddlery and a white under blanket, his hoofs were jet black and polished with oil.

This was a nobleman's horse Jervis said to himself. A pair of aldermen bought a wooden stool next to the horse, the King stood on the stool and the aldermen man handled him onto the horse, sitting still on the horses back he signalled to the men that he was settled, the Aldermen removed the stool and bowed low.

The horse strode away along the edge of the hill, then turned and came back, the King was surveying the battlefield

Thomas said "come brother should we not now go, Jervis said we wait for a while, we can see the battlefeld from here, look Thomas", Thomas sat on his long coat to get some comfort beneath his backside, Jervis was pointing to the left of Anne Beame Hill there in the misty and now smoke-filled distance were hordes of men, soldiers with a different standard these were the men they had seen the day before passing along the Barton lanes.

Northumbrian men rank and ranks of them they were attired with armour and long pikes, they were flanked by men on horseback heavily armoured. They spread out and down to the left of the vale, then stood their ground.

The drumming from the hill continued faster and more drummers were joining in, their beats were followed by the bellows of the trumpets and horns offering echoes across the vale, the sounds were getting louder and more frequent, on the far side of the vale near the roman road there massed an army of many more men, they in turn, drummed the arrival through the dadlyngton marches of more household archers and pikemen.

They had arrived on foot after a long march from Leicester were moving towards the vale centre along the Fenn lane, two men wide and as long as the lane would stretch, more men were descending from dadlyngton, some were moving along the edge of the hill at dadlyngton and rounding its slopes ten men deep and the stretch of almost a ½ mile along to Stoke Golding and further across to Shenton and Sandy-fford.

From the hill canon fire was being shot towards the oncoming marching army, these were not a serious attempt to kill, but early warning shots, a gauging of distance, but still a long way short of the advancing hordes, the canon smoke filled the treetops screening the view across the vale.

Thomas saw many canons being set besides the edges of the long marsh fields and at the edges of the wooded meadows, aiming their guns barrels towards land in between the lanes running away from and along the front of Anne Beame hill. Most of the lanes leading to the battlefield areas were gridlocked with Soldiers.

The intense regular, monotonous drumming was getting louder and deeper in its menacing call to arms, the air around was warming up, the sounds were travelling further across the flat vale.

Men at the rear of the hill were still eating and drinking a breakfast ale, meats of mutton and venison, duck and boar were being roasted, barrels of fish and pilchards were open covered in flies.

The stinking fish were served four to each platter, biscuits were stuffed into pockets and offered to every man, after eating each man was offered a blessing from a priest then in turn, each rank would ascend to the side of the hill and take their positions on the leading edge of the slope.

What faced them at every moment was a frightening view of 1,000's of men approaching from the southwest.

Their own outline in the rising sun was one of shining armour, the glint of pikestaff, halberds pikes and staves, 1000 archers 100,000 arrows, 2000, pikemen, 120 canons and their artillery men piles of cannon balls and chain balls set ready to fire across the battlefield as the enemy crossed in front of them.

200 mounted drummers joined in on the crescendo of noise now rolling around the vale over 2 miles in any direction. The fanfare of trumpeters shouting the come on to Henry the Tudor from the top of Anne Beame hill gave an eerie war cry.

CHAPTER 11

Back In Carltonstone, Clara heard a gentle knock at the door, she left the boy in his bed and wander down opening the door expecting to see Anna or better Jervis, there stood a man, she recognised him from the river bank, "what do you want"? she said half closing the door," I wanted your husband for business," replied the huge man "he is not here now" Clara responded, "he will be back later he has other business to attend to today," "I see" said the man in a foreign accent, "thank you" he said looking at her as he bowed and removed his cap from his head.

He took a step back and Clara closed the door, she turned and was returning to the boy, she heard something behind her, she turned around only to feel the grip of the man suddenly grab her, he had let himself back n to the cottage and held her by the neck holding his hand over her mouth, "Shut up" he commanded "be very quiet". She tried to turn and face him, but he pushed her towards the fireplace, he was strong and pushed her head hard against the mantle.

"You know what I want" he grunted in her ear, Clara shuddered as the man was sniffing her neck and hair, "what do you want ?" she said as her voice broke, "I want you" he replied, he was running his hands down her body, he started to kiss her hair breathing heavily as he held her tighter, "where can we go for some favour" he said , "Favour?" Clara replied, "I do you no favour get out of my home", Clara struggled and tried to pull away from him, he held her tight and was hurting her wrists, "get off me" she insisted.

"Your husband is not here we can have some favour and comfort, no? some simple venal sin for you, yes? feel me, I am here for you No?"

Clara shouted, "get off me this is a mortal sin I am a virtuous wife; you are trespassing his home and his wife my husband will kill you".

He laughed and said, "Then it is decided I will kill him first, come on Clara, I have been watching you for a while, you are a good woman, and you tease me so". Clara continued to struggle "I do not tease you, how do you know how to address me by my name, you are trespassing ", Clara shifted her stance and pulled her mouth away an bit down on the man's hand, he recoiled with a slap across her face, he pulled away, Clara manged to make some steps up the small set of stairs, the man followed her grabbing at her skirt, and pulling her back, she pulled away again as he missed his stepping.

Clara made it up to the top floor, "so you want to play games with hard to get you Clara" he shouted, as he ascended the steps on the stairs in pursuit, the blade of a halberd met his chest, there at the top of the stairs was Clara's son John, "do you want to feel how good my father is at blade sharpening ?" he said "I was told to protect my mother from harm and today I will.

The stocky man smiled and laughed at the boy,

"when I have finished with your mother Clara perhaps I can and have my satisfaction with you boy!".

 The man looked up at the boy for you are just a rag boy, no?" said the man laughing "you will have to face this English blade first foreigner"! said John moving forward and taking a stance.

"Now do as you have been advised and go from here, my father is on his way now, he will be here before you can show anyone if you are honourable. So go before I cut you down", John was raging with anger, he was shaking with nervousness and aggression, Clara was standing behind him.

She had a knife behind her back and was ready to defend her and her son. She screamed again at the man "Go! go Now!"

"Go from here and leave this place", Clara screamed, the man took a step down from the stair well, he turned half way to turn back down, John had the halberd pointed directly at the man's chest, the man made a grab for the pike, John was quick to lift it up and bought it down on the man's shoulder the blade was indeed sharp and cut into the man's tunic, the man lunged forward towards john in an attempt to grab the weapon.

John pulled the sharp blade up and poked the

man with all his might in the chest with the tip, he fell backwards and fell over and down the last few steps falling on the floor, the blade had stabbed him in the chest, blood was coming from the tunic and was turning red, "Go! Shouted John and Clara together.

There was a loud knock to the door and Anna and William Barker stood there, they had heard the shouting and commotion, what the? William said.

The man got up and pushed past the two, he jumped the wicker gates and ran across the perches at the back of the cottage and away across the river.

Clara! Are you alright" called Anna, what in lords name has happened? Clara took hold of John and gave him a long hug, "where is your father?" she whispered in John's ear, "you are my soldier". "I am thankful you turned up, John was ready to run the man through he was so brave" Clara was in tears and shaking with fear but thanks to the bravery of her son , she was shaken but unharmed.

Clara and Anna thanked William for his help and asked that nothing should be said to Jervis until Clara and Anna had spoken to him, William said I will not discuss with anybody he agreed, William walked to the back of the cottages and looked across the river, there was no sign of the man. He returned to his home trudging through the mud in the lane.

Anna said to Clara, "there is a battle close by our men have gone to see it , these French men will be everywhere, we should take the cart and take the children to Smisby and my cousin Joshua", Anna said "I agree Clara, I see that is a safe thing we will be a target for this type of thing, if word gets out that our husbands are away, we can be back tonight or tomorrow Anna said, yes let us get the children we will take the cart and some food with us, Clara said I will prepare food,!" Clara asked John "can you get the horse ready and put her to the cart", "I will mother," said John.

He went off to attend to the horse, Anna went to the Peter at the chapel and told him of their plan, he said he would tell Jervis when the brothers returned.

Soon John had the cart hitched to the horse and ready, Anna loaded her 3 children into the back of the cart and covered them with a canvas, "this will keep you dry if the lord sends us more rain." The children thought this was a great adventure and were enjoying themselves.

Clara arrived and stepped on to the cart, John started to pull away then stopped, "wait" he said," I will be back", he jumped down and ran into the yard he pulled back a cover and came back with his pike and blade.

He put them in the back of the cart. He took the reins and pulled away, the 6 of them slowly made their way towards the roman road and onwards to Smisby.

CHAPTER 12

"Sir you will receive bare tha' vile colours of tha't thyre rag of shite off mine own sov'rign lande".

Thomas and Jervis had not said a word to each other for a long spell, they had been watching the developments below and afar, the smell coming across the lanes and field leading to Ann bean hill were sweet , sometimes foul the air was full of spice and the smell of roasted meat from the war kitchens , horse piss and shit were a mire in the lanes below where Thomas and Jervis as the morning warmed the air where they were hiding, was acrid and unpleasant, Jervis said shall we depart?

Thomas said "yes we should go before this war gets underway", the two brothers started to shin down the trunk of the tree, they immediately became aware that soldiers were approaching , another rank of dirty mercenary troops turned the corner, quickly Jervis called gesticulating to go back up into the tree Thomas said "go back up the tree", they scrambled back up as they did Thomas dropped his arrows from his leather belt, they tumbled down and landed at the feet of the lead soldier, he stopped and looked left and right, he stopped the column of men behind him holding up his long halberd. The ranks behind him stopped on an uncertain shuffle of boots.

As they stood there in mire of shitty mess, he ordered a man from the front of the march to pick the arrows up, they were covered in a stinking mess.

At long range, a shit encrusted arrowhead or bodkin was a dangerous injury, if the skin was broken, the festering of the wounds especially in a warm summer would soon bring infection, this would undoubtedly lead to a fever and a long lingering death. "We shall take some satisfaction with these errant bow pokes," said the soldier. He passed them back into the rank of archers and long bowmen, the rank of Soldiers marched on past towards the hill.

Thomas and Jervis were holding their breath in the tree, Jervis suggested they try and climb higher, the tree cover was a little thicker they would be better covered from being discovered from the ground and they would be able to see more. Jervis had lost track of the moment he was enthused to stay and see the battle commence; it was clear the two brothers had no idea of the ferocity and terror of the battle ahead.

They scrambled and climbed up to almost the canopy of the two big trees, Thomas sat in the crook of a branch, Jervis found a settle in the canopy and Thomas sat in the branches high above the roadway, there he had a clear view of the mélange below.

The trumpeters were sounding off a squeal of a sound, some would have said it was uncomforting to the ears. It went on continuously for a long while. The drumming from Anne Beame hill was fast and hard and extremely loud, something is happening Brother called Thomas to Jervis. The top of the hill was occupied by a large contingent of heavy military horses, each man had a standard and full armour.

The Short man who Jervis said and had guessed was the King was standing next to a magnificently decorated and armoured horse, long leather straps shielded the legs of the animal, the saddle was embellished with fine leather carving, the reins were gilded with woven hand holds and a hood to shield the horses' eyes.

He stood there chin raised , in his fine armour resplendent in his garb of brightly polished royal Sallet and Bevor, topped with his circlet crown, his hands on his hips surveying the flat marshy land in front of him, the Hill was about 350 feet above sea level so his view of the 1000's of soldiers assembled, was all seeing, from the Dadlyngton side he could see the approaching enemy, from the area of the roman road he could see the armies of William Stanley in waiting.

The King had control of three sides Anne Beame hill to Sutton to Shenton and opposition covered a similar stretch of countryside, they in turn had Dadlyngton across to Whitemoor and the central part of the vale just off the roman road to the southwest. In the middle of the vales and flat countryside was a spinney, on the far reaches of it was a pond and reeded marsh.

Scattered across this area were some large boulders and rocks. The Duke of Northumberland galloped to the top of the hill and dismounted, he approached the King and bowed before him, they exchanged words, and both were pointing toward the men now assembled at the bottom of the hill, the King waved his arms, and the duke re mounted to join his men some way off.

Below in the vale the mists had cleared, smoke now enveloped the countryside, peeling off as it crossed the hillside at Anne Beame Hill and over to the Whitemoor it filtered away like a ghostly vail. Soldiers were still assembling below, as Jervis and Thomas continued to keep out of sight, further down the lane they could see other local men climbing the trees to gather a view of the colour and pomp on the vales and side marsh.

Another volley of cannon fire was thrown onto the Fenn fields great clouds of acrid sulphurous smoke drifted into the trees where Thomas and Jervis were clinging on to the treetops, the smell was debilitating and left both men with streaming eyes and burning throat.

A loud fanfare sounded out across the field, the trumpeted sounds were long and almost breath bustlingly continuous, then silence just a faint echo across the vale, nothing, no dogs barking, no drumbeats. A cool breeze was felt on the brothers' cheeks, both looked on in trepidation and silence, as it was clear something was to happen this may be the beginning Jervis said to his brother.

Jervis looked across to the top of the hill, the King was now on his horse, resplendent in battle dress and armour, astride a horse of some heritage, it was 18 hands tall, broad, powerful looking animal, it stood still not a flinch from its flanks.

The King raised it sword from the saddle scabbard, he held it high, from a half a mile away could be heard horses galloping on firm ground, over the thudding of the galloping could be heard men shouting and screaming, this was an army of angry determined men, from beyond the brush line the colours of the opposition came into view, and like a thunderstorm approaching, the noise increased.

The King on his horseback dropped his sword, a shout went out, and 1000 archers shot 1000 arrows into the air, the combined sound of the arrows being launch together was ear piercingly loud, it sounded like a whip cutting through the air, some of the arrows found their target as the approaching horsemen were cut down by the barrage of incoming bodkin heavy arrows landed amidst the gallop, some injuring horses, in the neck and the hind quarters the horses falling to the ground and dismounting their heavy rider.

Some of the arrows hit the mounted chargers in the arms legs and backs, horses reared up men screamed out the 100 horsemen were cut down to 70 or 80.

Back on the hill the archers quickly reloaded, the King raised his sword again and so did another commanding soldier on horseback, he watched for the King to drop his sword, after a few moments the archers were given another call, this time instead of firing into the air the aimed directly at the approaching hordes.

The swoosh sound was powerful and frightening, as the bodkins split the air as they volley forward raining down on the approaching horsemen, these were long bowmen their bows were 6 feet tall.

As tall as a man, the bowman was strong, they had trained since youngsters to fire these ash yew and willow bows.

English longbow archers were often deformed from years of archery! The high poundage of war bows, coupled with years of training in their use from a young age, led to archers having developed larger shoulder muscle and arm bones to compensate for the growth of physic around those areas.

The arrows quickly found their mark again the front line of the horsemen making their way towards the hill were again cut down and horses grounded , the Archers reloaded again, the attackers were now only 50 of the 100 that started out, the Other commander on horseback from the hill shouted , he had a pike and halberd under his arms , he moved down the flanks of the hill and started a charge toward the attacker, he was followed by 120 horsemen, they clashed hard into contact with the attacking enemy and the clanking of sword and halberds pikes and poke made a sickly thud as leather and steel met and they found an entry point into the armour.

Flesh wounds to the head and legs were deadly combined with head injuries and the worst of blood and gore, could be seen flowing from the vantage point on top of the hill, as the Yorkist's rampaged their way into the swirling skirmish, cutting down one horseman after another.

Horses were screaming as they were slaughtered, the attackers gave a valiant fight, but this was only the first fight of the day. The Lancastrians made a retreat the field was strewn with bodies, limping men, injured horses, blood, and guts severed arms and hands, some men just sat there in a shock and dazed condition.

The Yorkist's returned to the hill a few of them trotted around the field, trampling the half dead to death, swiping at those dazed and injured putting them to a pathetic death with humiliation, shouting obscenities at them before dispatching them with the swipe of the halberd or sword, some men totally and mentally dazed or bleeding so much shock had set in, and the mercy of a quick death was a way they believed to the Lord almost demanded by those injured enough to warrant a killing of mercy. Soon the battlefield returned to a silence, the cries of some thought to be dead or not worth the effort in the field could still be heard.

A battalion of men from the Anne Beame hill marched forward and down the flanks of the hill, they stood with swords drawn and bows loaded, these were the mercenary men bought to the battle with money taken from Notting-hamshire and Leicestershire as alms payments, or shield money.

A fanfare sounded out again accompanied by the drumming again, this went on for some time. This time is was the menace in its haunt-ing sounds, the Yorkists revelling in the Lancas-trian retreat, the blood stained battlefield was only just cleared of dead or wounded horse and the two sides became set to charge each other again.

A series of booms from the cannon fire called an immediate end to the fanfares it arrived loudly but not from the hill, canon ball came ripping through the flanks of men many dived for the ground as the cannon balls of stone and lead tore through the trees and hedge, some of the cannon balls disintegrated as they flew through the air the result was a strafing of more of the enemy, scattering horses startled by the com-motion caused, men dived for cover, and pro-tection in the long marsh grasses surrounding the area, only one or two men were taken down the majority stood tall again, shouting at the opposition one quarter of a long mile away.

The retreating men from the previous charge had regrouped and were in groups deep in dis-cussion with the next wave getting ready to charge into the field, some 200 horsemen from the Yorkist's were mounted , they were angry men the King would ride into battle with them, albeit surrounded by the Kings men, a protective group who would fight with him but were there to offer another layer of protection for his majesty's horse, if the Kings horse was un injured at any time then the King would have a means of escape from any battle field. These Kings men were trained to protect the horse of the Kings as much as the King himself.

The battle was now in full, between the two warring sides was the marsh, but the Earl of Oxford, at the vanguard of Henry's army, moved around this, now avoiding the cannon fire and the trees around the march shielding them from Richard's cannons. Keeping the marsh on his right he attacked the Duke of Norfolk. On the vale before Dadlyngton hill, A fierce battle ensued with Oxford's men getting the upper hand.

A troop of soldiers marched onto the battlefield from the far side of Whitemoor on the left flank was a tall standard bearer he carried an enormous standard; this was no ordinary standard bearer it was that in the hands of Sir William Brandon the tallest man on the battlefield.

The King said to his general Lord General Oxford,

"Sir you will receive bare tha' vile colours of tha't thyre rag of shite off mine own sov'rign lande".

Sire, take the colours it is for yourself we will abide by your side in a gallop", the King looked and raised an eyebrow and a smile, it will be my own and gods wish my lord. They had then noticed that Henry had become distanced from his bodyguard, thinking he could kill his rival, he gathered a posse of men, his personal retinue, and charged around the melee that was going on and was going for Tudor himself.

The King raised his sword again as the hordes approached, some on horseback and some on foot, the Yorkist's troops gathered at the right-hand flank remained out of view.

It was of that'd witness 'ed of n'rfolk's men anon did start to fleeth the battlefield. Witness to this Richard deploy'd n'rthumb'rland's sizeable contingent to fight, but aft'r having given the 'rd'r the n'rthumb'rland men satteth Th're and didst nothing.

The King called on top of his voice the charge, "For God and mine own Country" and off galloped 30 horsemen, led from the front by the diminutive hunchback of Richard III, he circled the rear of his charge he could see his own standard bearer an enormous man Sir William

Brandon to his right, beyond he could see Henry Tudor surrounded by mounted soldiers on the lower flanks of the hump at Dadlyngton windmill, he tracked back, surrounded by his cohort of protective lords and commanders, they swelled forward into the clash, it was violent, intense grewsome, bloody, stabbings were everywhere the blood and fighting was hot and sticky vile work, hand to hand face to face, fingers and hands were being cut fingers lost hand mutilated, a stab under the rib cage caused an immense amount of pain as the liver or heart were compromised leading to heavy haemorrhaging and the eventual loss of conciseness.

The King Richard encircled by halberds and pike heads the King made his way across the back of the battle and found in front of him William Brandon, Brandon was on foot having been dismounted from his horse, his standard being held high and a lose halberd making it difficult to manage the two so he was using the standard pole to defend himself, the line opened up there was before Richard was Henry Tudor albeit surrounded by Tudor Pikemen.

Death to the Tudor was in Richards eyes and actions he spared no mercy slicing into men and horses as he made his enraged way towards Brandon and further on Tudor, the King road his majestic horse fearlessly in toward Tudor between them stood Brandon, Richard charged at Brandon knocking him down with his silver tipped Lance, the King showed his excellent horsemanship and turned again on Brandon in a full speed gallop he knocked him to the ground again for a second time this time cutting his legs off beneath him, the King rode back again to see Brandon composing himself as he reached for the standard which had been knocked from his grip, as had his halberd the standard was laying now on the ground being trampled on by horses and men from both sides, the King rode back and in again into where Brandon had now got his back to the approaching King , the King reached for his Lance and shouting "be with you and your Tudor bastard lord off my sovereign soil you traitor" at that point he drove down his lance upon Brandon catching him under his armpit with such ferocious intent the Kings lance cut Brandon to the ground, the King had cut into his armour the lance splintering into his chest exposing flesh and sinews blood pumping from Brandon's torso.

Henry was nowhere to be seen, he was taken back at the sight before him, troubled by the death of his standard bearer and stunned at the gruesome sight of his own men being slaughtered. He had huddled into a group of his men and was being shielded from Richard III.

Amongst all other Knights, remember

**which were hardy, and thereto wight; Sir
William Brandon was one of those, King
Heneryes Standard he kept on height, and
vanted itt with manhood & might vntill
with dints he was driuen downe, he dyed
like an ancyent Knight, with HENERY
of England that ware the crowne.**

The Yorkist's King rode fast to the back of the flank of fighting men taking down some of the enemy as he rode past. Satisfied he had cut down the standard bearer the King and battle cohort returned to Ann Beame hill.

The view before Jervis and Thomas perched high in the treeline was one of carnage, men screaming for their loved ones, men screaming for their mothers, screaming for forgiveness, limbs dismembered arms hands heads corpses lay everywhere impaled on lances, halberds swords, pikes, nothing was unused in the pursuit of the death of the opponents.

Steaming horses some dead some cut down injured lame some squealing helpless on the field, some horses were roaming free some had set off to escape across the land beyond the battlefield.

The men returning from the field were bleeding cut some with cuts across their face's ears missing a disgusting litany of vile fighting methods where on the battlefield there were no rules it appeared to be only one of kill or be killed.

From the vanguard of Henry Tudor's forces, a big man on a horse was always at the back of Henry Tudor, he held a huge halberd and long sword. He didn't come into fight but was just held back in the rear of the assembled at Whitemoor.

The hurlyburly wast anon in full, between the two warring sides wast the marsh, but the earl of oxf'rd, at the vanguard of henry's army, hath moved 'round this, anon avoiding the cannon fireth from richard's cannons. Keeping the marsh on his right that gent did attack the duke of n'rfolk. On the vale bef're dadlyngton hill, a fi'rce hurlyburly ensu'd with oxf'rd's men getting the upp'r handeth.

Richard III made ready for another charge, the noise was still intense and confusing to those not privy to the rules of this engagement. Richard was keen to join in the next charge, his advisors said for him to take charge of the battle from the vantagepoint on Anne Beame hill, he refused, he was fired up angry Tudor had slipped past him,

Richard wanted to find him and with the lords wish in his fervently spinning in his head as he believed strongly and with no doubt that he was doing the said Lords work in ridding this evil from England,

He would dispatch him by himself, Richard soon found another lance, the called his trusted soldiers around him and rode down into the hell below, there he fought several fights one after the other and beat down the opponents easily for such a small man, as he moved left beating his way along the flanks the ground beneath his horse feet became softer, a mire of mud, blood and horses was where Richard found himself, slashing with his sword he made good progress along the edge of the marsh area, his confidant called to him to pull back from the marsh.

In the noise and shouting Richard didn't hear him, the horse faltered over a rock as Richard moved backward, the horse s legs folded, and a tree stump tripped the horse down and unseated Richard. The King was waist deep in filth and water, the water was dark red, running so with the blood of those dead and bleeding in the field. His horse was stymied, it was in a panic trying to release itself from the bog.

Immediately Henry, spotting Richard's awkward and untimely dismount despatched his men towards the place where Richard was now wading in the Marsh.

He was cursing the sky like a mad man; his ire and rage and complete anger belied the situation of him being vulnerable and with no horse.

One of Richards horsemen saw what was going on and went to rescue Richard, "Sire take my horse escape yourself from this before you are attacked, come get on my horse and let us see our way off", Richard replied with:

Richard shaking with anger and rage, gritting his teeth holding his sword vertical, blood of others streaming from his hands and across his forehead shouted to his cohort. Spitting and foaming at the mouth he bellowed:

"God f'rbid I yield one step from h're at th's battelfeld,

Pointing his sword at the assembled of his own men he continued:

"I shall greeteth mine own death with the lord, I as King, 'r cutteth tha' bastard Tudor down".

The group of men came around to protect Richard who was still wading around in the swamp mess of the marsh, to his left he found his horse still trying to get up, within a few moments the Tudor's men arrived and engaged in a fight with 6 of Richards men, they fought hard, cutting, and slashing with French swords and pike.

Soon after arrived 50 or so of Tudor's mercenaries, merciless men of death, they surrounded Richard's men and overpowered them and cut them down beheading two men and taking the legs off another two, the last man was run through, and his sword arm removed with one hack from a Frenchman's halberd.

Richard fought hard and from his single-handed disadvantage swiping at the aggressors growling at them as he used every part of his will and strength to fight away those who were all trying to get closer to Richard and being fought off.

More of Richard's soldiers arrived on foot to engage with the mercenaries one by one they were cut down leaving a shrinking band of Richards loyal soldiers, each one of Richard protectors were beaten back several yards away and the Tudor men viciously fought down Richard's cavalry,

An attack directed on Richard who was now surrounded, a slash with a halberd at Richard caught his armour and helmet knocking him down to his knees, a second blow came and knocked Richard down and over on his back again, a third blow was direct and so hard it knocked off his helmet and circlet crown and knocked Richard down into the muddy filth.

6 or 8 men piled in and overpowered Richard with clubs and fists raining down on him, he was for a moment knocked senseless, the a small group of four mercenaries men pulled him out of the mire by his legs and face first on to solid ground, there they took turns and kicked him in the head, and his back, his face and head disfigured by the torment, a volume of blood pouring from his nose and head wounds.

A tall man stepped forward and cut the leather strap from Richards sallet and removed his bevor with a sword, cutting Richard neck, ear and chin, his highly polished helmet was kicked from his head, by two soldiers.

The taller soldier stepped forward and put his foot on Richards neck another soldier ran forward and again kicked Richard's head grazing off his ear.

Richard cried out a whimper, in pain his guttural voice scream was garbled with blood in his mouth and throat. He lost consciousness again his body becoming limp and lifeless.

The tall man broad burly and strong stooped

down and shook Richard to rouse him from his stupor, a few moments later he shook him again and waited for Richard to start to moan and gain some consciousness, Richard for a few moments murmured some words from his swelled lacerated lips and bleeding tongue,

"in Gods nameth thee shall ent'r hell below f'r this unholy and unlawful ingress in to mine own sov'reign lands!"

It was mostly unintelligible, he screamed in pain and anger insults aimed to the men surrounding him. Richard couldn't see where the next blow was to come from, he had lost the sight from one eye blood and a patch of mud and silt covered his eye socket, but his other eye keenly focused on the big Welsh man Rhys ap Thomas, Richards one eye open wide, and his pupils fixed.

Richard started to yell again his gurgled and hoarse voice could hardly be heard, but he mumbled.

"f'r all those i has't did love and known, and may not knoweth beyond this day, shall avenge this h'resy, may thy life beest mis'rable and thy actions regrettable fr'm the hell burning thee shall taketh"

Staring on, shaking his head in a disbelief was the huge man, standing over him with a hateful stare, they didn't know each other there was no respect, no recognition of Richard as a man or a King or from Richard to his aggressor and enemy.

Rhys ap Thomas bent down and lifted the King up by his chest plate, he punched Richard squarely in the face at the same time dropping Richard down again like a rag doll.

Remove it from the cripple below! He pointed as he ordered a soldier close by, two men pulled the breast plate from Richard cutting the straps catching the back of Richard arms and ribs as they purposely cut deep.

Richard lay there one of his arms trapped under his back, a leg trapped under the other, Richard was almost hog tied by his own body weight and with no strength left, being unable to move.

Rhys ap Thomas stood towering over Richard's battered body amidst the chaos and war cries all around him, he looked around hands on his hips, at the battle roaring all around them.

Men were falling, blood was being let, the battle was killing men on each side, horses lay dead or dying, panting for help as they lay bleeding, arrows, Pike, and halberd long and short swords finding their way into flesh and bone.

Rhys ap Thomas looked down on the King Richard writhing in the mire desperately trying to free himself, he took a deep breath sucking snot up through his nose, he spat on Richard as a show of disgust, defiance, and disrespect. Richard's face was defiled in snot, blood and saliva, another soldier stomped on Richards left hand breaking his fingers.

The big man Rhys ap Thomas took one a purposeful step back and without looking back and keeping his eyes in contact with Richard who was almost drowning in the filthy water, reached to his long halberd being held by another solider to his left, the noise and screaming and cannon fire continued in the background.

The fighting still intense and men dying all around. Richard continued to scream at the top of his voice, protesting these men on his sovereign soils were here in defiance to the words of the Lord that his reign should ever be questioned.

The big man Rhys ap Thomas shouted down to Richard, "Richard, tyrant King of England listen to me, he called to Richard again and slapped his face, Richard, listen to me you broken fool, Richard focused with one eye at Rhys ap Thomas ap Griff, Richard listen to me you devil.

"Thy lif'es endeth is near, t is f'r anon
Richard and at which time it cometh,
You have seen tha't Henry Tudor is
clos'e at hande and that Lord and gent
and this army art h're to settle'th this
just quarrel 'gainst thee Richard,

f'r thou art the unnatural tyrant king of
yest'rday, I hath promised my Lord that with-
standing not a droplet of undoubtful blood is
to beest hath left in the kingdom of England
following this square and valorous battle.

"May the besste good god look upon you
and offer at beest thy judgeth thee evil
vile hunchbac and crippl'd tyrant".

Richard was attempting to make a reply, his
voice curdled with blood, snot and vomit, his
eye blinded now full of mud and filth.

Rhys ap Thomas took a step back, one of his
men close to him handed back his halberd, Rhys
ap Thomas took a careful look around him, the
battle was close by, he could hear the clash a few
100 yards away, he gazed down at the pathetic
man below him, what shall I do the Welshman
questioned himself, he waited a few moments
as Richard struggled.

Griff then raised his weapon high above his
head, he looked Richard squarely in the eye,

with all his might he raised the halberd and bought it down on the top of Richards head, it was a violent action meant without doubt to stop any man's life and in particular the life of Richard Plantagenet.

The crushing blow came swiftly and violently in one move. Richard's head was pushed backwards into the watery mud, blood immediately hissed like a fountain from the wound, Richards body contorted and curled up, Richard closed his eyes, his mouth moving but from came no words, he rolled over in a last wave of agonised sharp and terrible pain, Richards body contorted again, and he exhaled the contents of his gut, vomit spewed across Rhys ap Thomas's boots, It was almost a last final gift of a last word of defiance from Richard III.

Rhys ap Thomas raised his weapon again and bought its down on an attempt to behead the pathetic twisted body of Richard, as a trophy to be taken back to Henry, he missed, the blow was ferocious, it with one blow cut and sliced the back of Richard's head, the blood and the contents of his skull spilled out.

Richards hands were raised and flailing like a demented puppet, all six men stood back as the life left Richard Plantagenets body.

 What was immediately before them was a

small pathetic broken body, it now had stopped moving, his mouth was open his neck contorted backwards from Rhys ap Thomas second blow, his eyes remained open, staring with a lifeless empty gaze at the men who had in a moment taken his life and kingdom who were assembled above him, the face of Richard was now pale and grey his fingers shattered and blooded within his armoured gauntlet, and his legs bent upward toward his deformed and broken spine.

Rhys ap Thomas turned and signalled to the front line of the waiting Tudor men, they made their way across to the marsh edge where Richards body lay.

Henry Tudor at the rear was amongst them, he arrived flanked by lords and protectors, he came to a halt some yards from the gruesome scene before him, some of the others cheered as the battle around them was still in full Ire from both sides.

Henry Tudor's horse took a few steps forward and stopped, Henry looked on and down at the pathetic sight of the broken and bloodied body of Richard. a look of shock was apparent on his face, he was lost for words Henry Tudor didn't expect this scene of murder and death, this was not his world he was not used to the business of the battlefield and death, he had thought Richard would be captured, sent to London to be tried and executed.

Henry bowed his head and said a quiet prayer asking for forgiveness as a witness to the butchery afforded to Richard Plantagenet. He looks so small for such a big king commented Henry.

Rhys ap Thomas stood there and looking down at the body before them, "he is no more my lord "said Rhys ap Thomas.

"Did he fight well?" asked Henry Tudor, "He fought valiantly my lord,

Rhys turned to look at Henry directly "He fought well and as a true man, here before me and by my hand has died quickly but badly," said Rhys ap Thomas.

It is over Rhys said. "It is and this is the work of the lord" said Henry Tudor, "I am now realised the day before this day and now as the rightful King of this land".

Rhys ap Thomas instructed one of his men to find Richard's horse, a few men went to pull the distraught animal from the bog mud and marsh, they came back with it sometime later, it had become trapped by a submerged tree trunk. But when released was unfettered by the scene, the loyal horse remained calm and stood next to Richards discarded body.

A lord on his horse flanked by 8 outriders approached, Henry's men stood firm with pikes and halberds swords and daggers drawn they in a protective move circled Henry, he called to his men to stand aside, Henry's men stood down and let Sir William Stanley approach.

This is a murderous sight Lord Henry, it is replied to Henry, but I now stand before you as the victor, now do you work with me Sir? asked Henry, I am at your service Sire and will offer you my loyal support and my men.

Sir William bowed from the saddle of his horse, Henry nodded in recognition, he said to Sir William, "William, we have our agreement, for your part I call upon you to clear this field and make fast the rout for those unwilling to yield. I will Sire said William Stanley.

The blood and stench coming from Richards body was gut wrenchingly unpleasant, his face was disfigured, and his head cut almost in half. Henry instructed Rhys ap Thomas's men to strip Richards body naked.

Four men bent down, with no hesitation they ripped the fine clothes from Richard's limp blood-stained body, putting away into their own pockets Richard tunic and contents of his bag.

Men! called Henry, Have respect for this man!

Henry nodded to all of them individually. Sire shall we cover his head to hide his injury? No leave him naked as he came into this world, for all men folk to see.

He gave the order that Richard will re-enter the city from where he rode into battle, To swine tie the corpse to the horse and parade it back to Leicester via Newark, instruct the soldiers of Richard Plantagenet to either heed and surrender and give true allegiance to the new King or, if it is their choosing then may God have mercy, then they will to run for their life, pursue everyman that runs away from this day and strike them down in the name of the Lord and the King. For the King is now dead, and I am the King.

News of the death of Richard and his fall was travelling quickly across the battlefield, some of his soldiers looking back in disbelief despite the battle was now in full flow, defeat of the Yorkists was in hand and soon men were leaving the fields and making off.

Between the two warring sides besides the marsh where Richard lay lifeless and pathetically laid out, the Earl of Oxford, at the vanguard of Henry's army, moved around the marsh, now avoiding the cannon fire from Richard's cannons on the flanks of Anne Beame Hill.

Keeping the marsh on his right he attacked the Duke of Norfolk. soldiers looking on to the edge of the marsh, many men witnessing this man-oeuvre started to leave the battlefield, the lanes were starting to fill up with men running aside riderless horses galloping away.

Jervis was holding on tight as he stood aloft on the tree branch said across to Thomas something happened by those marshes brother, Thomas I could see witness to what has happened, look the battlefield was starting to break up, men on the edge of the field were dropping their shield s and making off they were fleeing from all over the field, we will have to make our way safely out of here said Thomas, we could get caught up in this running, come brother let us get down from here. let us think of a safer way home.

CHAPTER 13

"The hurly-burly wast anon in full, between
the two warring sides wast the marsh,
but the earl of oxf'rd, at the vanguard of
henry's army, hath moved 'round this, anon
avoiding the cannon fireth from Richards'
cannons. Keeping the marsh on his right
that gent did attack the duke of n'rfolk.

On the vale beff're dadlyngton hill, a fi'rce hurly-burly ensu'd with oxf'rd's men getting the upp'r handeth.

On the far side of the battlefield Lord Sir William Stanley seeing the men surrounding where Richard was last seen entered the battle, he did not order his men to fight for Richard's side but for Henry Tudor, who was his stepson.

King Richard had taken Stanley's son hostage before the battle to ensure his loyalty, this was a form of payback by Stanley, although Stanley at this point didn't know Richard was dead. His army of men chased the battle blooded Richards men from the field they ran north and west across the open field marshes and woodlands.

Not that now it mattered but Richard may not have known before he was killed that Henry had met with William Stanley that morning, but it certainly seems that he did not trust Stanley's loyalty. The orders were clear however that should Stanley fight for Henry his son would be put to a quick death on Richards orders. This order was not carried out.

William Stanley arrived at the marsh side to greet Henry ,he witnessed the gruesome scene, A welcome was given to Henry as the sovereign King, he then turned , he rode back to the battle line, and engaged Richards remaining men, he took control of the battle which continued for a good while, men from both sides were continually being killed and maimed, it took several hours for all the fighting to stop, even then skirmishes broke out in lanes and fields as the valiant side made their way north to Leicester and Lincoln Tamworth and Derby and Nottingham.

The y'rkists men in tha days of beff're
Square fought hand to hand in a
stench of blud and go're.
All believ'rs did trust in justice are endorsed.
They'd hath followed that King
th're just and of because.
Rememb'r well men who is't to tha Anne
Beame on a hill, hath passed this way.
Souls of men alive bef're the misty blued
dawn on the augustine 22nd day
'Gainst Henry's odds those gents
wouldst not lay down nor yield.
The hath lost souls of men who is't death
did come on the run from redemo'r feld.

The two brothers climbed down from the trees, Thomas lost his grip and fell the last few feet and fell hard on his ankle, he cried out to

Jervis, who took him by the arm, he dragged him into the woods, Thomas was limping badly Jervis pulled him hard Thomas making a noise of complaints as he did, "be silent brother!" insisted Jervis. Jarvis's father once said of Jervis "that boy was born without patience or tolerance."

"I have hurt my ankle brother", Jervis stopped and pulled Thomas closer, "look at me Thomas, stop crying and realise, it is your ankle or your life! now shut up!" Jervis shook his brother, Thomas cowering from his brother had realised this was now life or death.

They made their way hidden by the beds of nettles and ferns as they ran back into the woods, they kept low and out of sight, they walked and scurried through the wood, trying to keep their heads down low, hiding from tree to tree.

Vast beds and bushes of nettles and ferns were they're only heeding as they beat them down and slowly made their way west back toward Carltonstone.

Following the treeline and staying out of the way of other people fleeing the area, as Jervis stopped, he pointed across the fields, there in plain sight were men making their escape and throwing away their helmets and armour letting the horses go and making for the north or the east.

A Horse galloped past the lane, Thomas and Jervis could hear its hoofs clattering along, as it did the armoured rider was shouting:

**"White lilied cowards runneth f'r thy
life f'r i shall taketh thy red blood"**

The rider looked to his left and spotted the two brothers walking briskly through the glade of woods, he shouted across to the brothers.

"Running hence as coward's art thee!"
"Aaaagggh Ill cut thee down".!

The soldier shouted from his grey horse. Waving his sword, he turned across the hedge line and into the woods,

Without saying a word or looking at each other the two brothers started to run.

Thomas in pain from his injured ankle took off running in one direction, over the wooden bridge at the Sandyfford the horseman following him, 90 paces behind.

Jervis took off in another direction, Jervis ran for his life, the horseman continued to chase Thomas, Jervis followed but had ran to the right so the rider might not have seen him.

Thomas's heart was beating so fast he could

hardly catch his breath, he was scared that the soldier might catch up with him but also the horseman might cut and maim or even worse kill Thomas, all that was in his mind was" he wasn't supposed to have come to the battlefield.

Ahead of him was the small wooden bridge over the Sandyfford stream, the recent heavy rain meant the stream was in flood and the water level almost at the top of the foot bridge and flowing fast.

Thomas looked back to see the horseman in the darkness of the woods, he was still heading Thomas's way, Thomas looked into the water then at the bridge, he jumped into the waters just a short step from the foot bridge and behind a small spinney of young trees,

The water had a particular stench to it, sweet and gut turning, but it presented some refuge as the flow was fast and the depth such that he could hide.

Thomas waded through the edge of the stream, there were some reeds right next to the foot bridge, he hunkered down into the reed bed. The water was cool but stank foul, He kept still the sound of the water rippling by was all he could hear.

Then the familiar thump, thump of a canter on the ground of the approaching horseman and his heavy horse became louder, he just could see the top of the rider's helmet, Thomas took a deep breath then stooped down into the water and moved under the bridge, there he had a little space at the far side of the bridge, he moved backwards trying to find the bank, he almost fell down when his back came into contact with the bank of the stream under the bridge.

Something touched his leg.

He froze still in the stream of water which was at this point trying to push him from under the bridge into the main stream, I thought that if he did move with the flow would expose him to the approaching soldier, he slowly he put his hand down , what was touching his leg was a dead weight pushing against him, Thomas immediately thought it was a leather bag, he grabbed at it trying to get a grip of it, it was heavy and hard to move, he pulled it up toward his head the water was pushing the object towards him and it took all his strength to hold on with one hand and bring this thing up, he pulled on the object and it broke the water and there facing him was the body of a dead man, his face cut and eyes dead but open.,

Thomas almost choked at the sight and tried to push it away, but the flow of the water pushed it back into his face, the cold dead weight corpse was stuck, its foot was jammed in the brace of the wooden bridge, Thomas held his breath, he heard the horseman trotting up and down the stream, shouting "come out coward".

Thomas took hold of the corpses foot and twisted it to try and release it from the grip of the wooden bridge it was stuck fast.

The horseman made his way back toward the bridge crossing, Thomas ducked under the water, the lifeless grey faced body looking straight back at him in the murky blood-filled water.

Thomas did all he could not to vomit, he closed his eyes and concentrated on the foot of the dead man in front of him, eventually without looking Thomas managed to slip the boot off and the corpse slowly floated away, bumping from under the bridge line , the soldier seeing the corpse floating away from him down the stream, He said "Ah so there you are Yorkist bastard, I see thee now killed justly and drowned like a rat, it is not a good day to be a Yorkist! He bellowed a laugh, The horse stepped across the bridge, he stopped for a few moments, then with a kick from his spurs galloped across the scrubland field towards the woods again.

Jervis was now a good way through the woods and was still making his best way to get away; he could see the mounted soldier struggling to get through the woods and dense nettle beds; however, Jervis couldn't see Thomas anywhere and was concerned.

He hoped and assumed Thomas had used his senses and had gone to ground and not come to a bloody end at the hand of the Tudor horseman.

Jervis stopped and stood on a log there he could see over the edge of the wood and over the fields, he couldn't see Thomas, he could see the soldier, clearly a skilled horseman, he was turning back on himself and moving about the woods looking for more men fleeing the battlefield, he was making for an ambush for any man straying from the battlefields into the woods,

Jervis looked around for a place to hide, there was an exceptionally large old Oak tree with a burnt-out trunk on the other track to get to it, he had to cross the trail in the woods and make his way across the wood through a thicket of nettles and brambles. It wouldn't be long before the rider would be in this part of the woods, Jervis thought fast and looked back at the rider.

In the blink of his eye, he made a guess that he could make it, off he set, the rider on horseback had entered the wood trail, he had spotted Jervis's movements and made directly for him.

Jervis could hear the horse snorting as it approached, he was 80 or 90 paces away, Jervis Jumped across the thicket and rolled into another trail, he ran keeping low and made it to the big tree, he thought he could use the tree for cover and keep the Soldier at bay, he scrambled deep into the centre of the tree it making the best use of the huge proportions of the mighty Oak , he circled the enormous tree and found the back of it was burnt out enough to hide a man inside, he quickly tried to get into the cavity inside, looking up he could see daylight from above, getting hold using his hands and feet he scrambled up inside the tree trunk it was black and wet inside, his footing was lost a couple of time but the blind panic drove him deep inside and aloft.

Jervis could hear the gallop of the rider on his horse, the Oak tree and the surrounding ground thudded and vibrated, the horse galloped by and stopped close by the big tree log, Jervis could hear the horses breathing, he could smell the horse's breath as it paced up and down and around the tree trunk. There was rough ground around the base of the tree, lots of holes and soil mashed up by badgers sets below there.

The rider circled the tree trunk, unable to get closer due to the rough ground, his halberd held at the ready under his right arm as he led the horse in circles with his left hand on the reins.

I smell you" said the soldier, I smell you like a pox ridden rat. Jervis recoiled even further up into the hole in the trunk "Take heed you cowardly Yorkist peasant I will return for your gizzards".

The soldier faltered for a while whilst his horse became entangled amidst the roots of an old fallen tree covered by brambles and vines.

Jervis became aware that he was gripping his hands so tightly his arms were tingling. He was covered in nettle stings his arms and back were on fire with the rash of the stinging nettle. His heart was racing, and he was sweating so much the sweat was in his eyes and ears stinging, he was so scared he dare not move or make a sound.

In the distance through the branches and greenery of the woods in front of him Jervis could hear the cries and screams of men, Jervis looked through a hole in the tree trunk, he could see past the soldier who he was able to see trotting away as the dim light inside the trunk allowed him a view into the woods. In the distance all but a few 100 yards, he could see the feet of men jiggling as they were hauled up tree's by their necks in random hangings, no trial, no arrest, just a savage degrading end to life, under the direction of the new King. Jervis looked on in horror, he hoped Thomas was far,

far away. He hoped for all his heart and Clara in his mind this was not to be his end, most of all he prayed the solider didn't return to burn him out of the tree.

He heard another voice, Jervis froze again, the sweat rolling down his face, he held his breath, the soldier replied, but Jervis didn't hear the exchange, then a loud thud, and a cry from the horse, as if the soldier has dismounted, Jervis could hear the horse gallop away.

Jervis was expecting at any time for the rider to start poking his sword or pike into the burnt out hollow where he was hiding, he could still hear the horse trotting away, Jervis was curled up in a tight inside the hollow, he was determined not to move , not to make a sound, he was shielded inside the tree, leaves and old branches from the old tree gave him good cover.

He heard someone shout at the horse, and a smack the horse it then galloped away, there was silence. Jervis kept himself hidden as tight as a he could in the black space high up, he had been lodged in the dirty sooty blackness. He soon became aware of the horse sniffing around where he was hiding, he tried to back himself up deeper.

"I know you are in there villager, come out and make your way", Jervis heard the words but didn't recognise the voice the thumping of his heart in his head was overpowering his sense of hearing, he looked out below him, slowly into the brighter light, there below him was another horse, he couldn't see the rider, but he heard the words again, "come on out and go home, come out and make your way you do not have an option". Jervis ws trying to listen, his heartbeat banging in his head, he listened again.

"You must go home, Jervis come now!", Jervis heard his name, he slowly moved to take another look at the horse, there looking up to him was a soldier on a horse it wasn't the same grey horse it was Richard Sharnford.

He was blooded and covered in slashes and cuts, a bloodstained shirt, on the ground nearby lay the body of the Tudor soldier who was chasing Jervis and Thomas, he had an arrow in his head, deep red blood was in a pool all around him, Jervis looked up to Richard. "Come Jervis you have a chance now Thomas is ahead of you keep to the hedge and keep to the woods, make your way back, come now Jervis".

Jervis crawled out of the hollow covered in black soot and grimy dirt and red soil, his skin on fire with cuts and stings from the brambles and nettles he had sprinted through and surrounding him.

"You are injured Richard Sharnford? "I am" he replied, "but I will recover, now go before the battlefield flees and the Rout comes this way, do you not hear me? go Jervis go!" Jervis started to walk quickly then he started to run.

Behind him was a crescendo of noise of fighting men, he turned to see Richard Sharnford trotting off to the left and back towards Ann Beame Hill.

"Jervis!" shouted Thomas from his watery hiding place in the ditch ahead, Jervis over here, it's good to see you brother said Jervis come we must go home, this is going to be a wild dog chase to come about very soon, we must hide well or get home.

We are ahead of the fighting brother said Thomas let us make for home and our family and safety. Thomas took hold of Jervis's arm as Jervis tried to free him from his hiding place "Jervis, I saw and touched a dead man, he was stuck under this bridge, I freed him, and the soldier thought it was me", said Thomas "you must not worry about that now, be thankful it may have saved your life Thomas", "help me im stuck in the mud and cannot free myself" Thomas said in a panic, Jervis bent down in the ditch next to the wooden bridge, Thomas was stuck fast in the slimy mud, it took some effort from both brothers to release Thomas from the grip of the muddy bank.

Jervis gripped his hands and slowly Thomas was freed. The holding of his brothers' hands bought home to Jervis how dangerous this place was, as swift retreat toward their home would be the best course of action from now on.

The two brothers made for the hedge line of the fields, they ran down the reaches of the river crossing where they could, they were a good long distance from the village.

More and more men and fighting men were joining them.

These were other villagers from surrounding places also watching the battle, who were now aware that the French army was chasing them out of the county or death was the alternative. Soon there were 80 or 90 men running along-side Jervis and Thomas, stay close Jervis said as they all ran in the same direction.

CHAPTER 14

Thomas was still soaking wet, his clothes were heavy and cumbersome he was getting out of breath, he called to Jervis asking for a rest, Jervis looked behind them the men running at the rear were being caught by 20 or so soldiers on horseback, each soldier was cutting men down as they chased them, stabbing most in the back as they were caught up with, some stabbing them in the legs, then as they fall following through with a slice of the halberd , then a trample of the horse.

Jervis was panicked by the scene he looked forward and to the right then the left, he grabbed Thomas by his shirt pulling him closer, he said to Thomas we must run south, come, Thomas didn't take time to answer he ran with his brother.

They jumped the stream, Thomas hesitated as he looked down at the water flowing past it too was flowing red with blood from the battlefield, a familiar foul-sweet smelling mixture of horse blood and the blood of the men dead or dying in the field beyond Anne Beame Hill, at that point Thomas had a stark realisation as what todays seeing of a spectacle had become and continued to develop into the killing fields, they had witnessed that morning.

He was ashamed to have been a witness to death and the slaying of good men and the killing of the King, he looked to Jervis who was looking shocked and desperate to get back to Clara and his son John. They could still hear soldiers shouting and baying the fleeing horde.

On the other side of the flooded stream, it was

muddy and boggy, they scrambled through it across a little spinney, of brambles black thorn bushes and hawthorn it tore and shredded their shirts and trousers ripping their arms and hands, they work their best the fight through it, but it was their only defence for the men following them.

They continued to run breathlessly and walk as fast as they could faltering at potholes and rabbit burrows and almost by mistake falling onto a field full of goats and sheep. They wandered from one corner to the other keeping their heads as low as they could, at the other end of the field there was a small wicker gate they passed through it.

Looking back, less men were following them. Jervis said they are still coming we must keep moving Thomas, "my head is about to burst open said Thomas, we need to drink".

Soon they found a drover's track, it was hedged high each side and provided cover, it would lead them to Atterton and Mythe then from thereover the small hill to Ratcliffe and on they could walk the tracks and lanes to Wellsborough and down across the field and woodland toward Carltonstone.

After a while they stopped for a rest, the noise from the battlefield was distant but they could

still hear it they could still hear men screaming, they found a spring coming from beneath
a large stone, they took turns in tasting it first
then drinking some, it tasted earthy, but it
was satisfactory to be a short drop of water to
quench a thirst.

Both brothers sat there speechless, they both
had felt and witnessed the touch to death this
morning, Jervis looked at Thomas and said are
you ready brother, all I want is to be with our
family as soon as we can.

The heat of the early afternoon was now apparent, the clouds overhead again gathering and
moving across the vale.

Thomas wept a little "I agree and wish for the
same brother, I feel we have been unwise to be
here today, I have lost my bow and you have lost
your sword too, we must make progress Jervis it
is past the middle of the day", be strong Thomas
come on let us walk on.

They both looked up to the sun it was hidden
by hazy grey cloud the temperature was soaring
and it was a long way to get back to Carltonstone.

The two-brothers set off walking steadily towards Upton they followed the drovers tracks
and found themselves insight of the battlefield
again looking down upon the vale they could

see for a distance and the amassed armies which were now scavenging the field.

Weapons were being collected, armour stripped from the dead and dying, anyone found alive was dispatched from misery the bodies of and boys and men identified as Henry Tudor's men we dragged onto flat ground and their body marked with a cross.

Richard's men were pulled onto a pile. A clergy man from Dadlyngton was saying a prayer for the dying. He moved about the corpses saying a prayer to each dead soldier, as he moved off his dedication was to be followed by those who would then scavenge the body for anything of petty value.

Nearby at Dadlyngton windmill Henry Tudor and William Stanley had met up, Henry Tudor surveyed the carnage before him, he gave orders for all of his valiant men to be given a burial where they fell, and a prayer said for them and their lost family it was not a concern as to who's side each soldier fought all men were under the guidance of God and as such they should be laid to rest as they died believing in god and the work he wanted of them on that day. Most of the Yorkists that could be identified were buried in mass graves.

"Beffore any gentle 'man who is't sw're

fealty to the King wouldst, notwithstanding
any previous attaind'r, beest secureth
in his prop'rty and p'rson."

One of the Stanley brothers came to Henry and
said he would be blessed to crown Henry King
of England, Henry in a celebratory handshake
took thanks and agreed, a party of Henry's advisors and the Stanley's rode on a short distance
to Stoke Golding, stopping by the windmill
upon the side of a hill overlooking the fields of
blood below.

Richard's circlet was recovered by a sidesman of
Sir William Stanley from the battlefield, it was
blessed by the priest from Stoke Golding and at
Stoke Golding Sir William Stanley placed it on
Henry Tudor head.

There were no cheers or celebration, Henry
addressed his close loyal confidants and
commanders it was a time of loss and joy
Henry said, we are valorous let us rejoice.

The King hath said,

tom'rrow shall be cometh with the m'rning

**shall bringeth a new light, a new m'rn and
a new day, visage the challenges, dissolve
the shite, liveth t' as thee w're meanteth
to, a healthy heart, lighte of spirit, a
fond smile f'r friends an cousins.**

**Rememb'r yond each day is yours,
and each one too sh'rt to ign're those
kind invitations and new desire.**

**so, holde tha in thy heart and gage
yourself not to wasteth a moment**

They quietly gave a short prayer of thanks and Henry gave a personal prayer of Gods thanks to his mother Lady Margaret Beaufort who was instrumental in the planning of Henry Tudor return to England and as Henry's devout mother and even from enforced confinement she managed to have been instrumental in the financing of the armies of the exiled King to be. At that spot in Stoke Golding on Crown Hill they pronounced that Henry Tudor was the King Henry VII of all England.

*To secure his hold on the throne, Henry had
declared himself, King by right of conquest
from 21 August 1485, the day before
Bosworth Field. Being sure he would be King
Henry's strategy was fortuitous following
Richard Plantagenets death and was the
true start of the Tudor reign in England.*

Henry had declared that anyone who had fought for Richard against him would be guilty of treason and Henry would by this charge would have his land and liberty removed Henry would be able to legally confiscate all the lands and property of Richard III, while restoring his own.

Jervis and Thomas walked steadily, Thomas still limping and Jervis keeping a few feet away from his brother who was smelling bad, his sackcloth breeches and jerkin were torn and stained with the mud from the stream, but the water drying out head left a stench.

They came across Seth from the village, he was hiding low along Upton lane, he said thank god it's you two he called, So, you too are on the run said Jervis, Seth was dirty and had lost his boots, not on the run I was coming to see what the commotion was and was met by men in the rout, "I've seen 20 or so men cut down and murdered, there are Tudor soldiers in Carlton-stone going house to house!".

"What"? said Thomas "we must make for Carlton now".

"All is well Thomas your wife and children have made off north to Smisby, Anna told me to tell you if I saw you, they were warned by a man on a horse, Clara has gone with them."

Jervis looked around the hilltop, they were surrounded by soldiers and men on the run and horses laid up in the lanes, "which way shall we go? asked Thomas, "we should make for Redemoor, then back down across the fields and woods to Carltonstone". "It might take a while," Seth said, "can I come with you?" "of course,", said Jervis."

The three men walked swiftly through the lanes criss crossing from one side of the Derby Road to the other, the rain had started again, it was heavy and cold too, soon Jervis was wet and getting cold.

A shivering Thomas had covered his head with his hood but was soaked through.

The three men walked on, it was muggy warm, it was easy to sweat, even though the rain had chilled them, a thirst was upon them.

CHAPTER 15

Soon they came on a hovel inside the hamlet of Sibson, the rover was in flood and almost across the lane leading up to Wellsborough. It was a small rambling disused cottage, hidden from the road by the overgrowth and brambles.

The shutters were closed, but the doors were open, and covered partially by a rose and brambles, they approached slowly Jervis called out, is there someone here? there was no reply, Thomas waved Jervis on to get closer, Seth hid some way off behind a thicket,

Jervis banged on the door, there still wasn't a reply, Jervis waved Thomas closer, Jervis poked his head around the doorway he called again hey!

There is no one here this is abandoned he called to Thomas, Thomas in turn beckoned Seth across, they slowly went inside in the darkness they could see it was ram shackled and dirty. No one had lived there for a long time. the doors were overgrown with weeds and vines, Jervis said there is a well I will get water for us.

Seth and Thomas explored the cottage, Jervis drew water from the well keeping a close eye on the weather and anyone approaching, all three took turns to gulp it down from the pale.

The water was cool and refreshing, Jervis said we are still a long way from Carltonstone, we must take some rest here and wait for the exit from the battle to pass by.

"Our family is at Smisby, and I hope are safe, and content with my cousin's hospitality and homeliness, at least we can be sure the children will be safe" said Thomas as he hobbled towards the door.

"My Ankle is sore Jervis, I need to rest it", can we take a time here?" do you want to go on Seth or are you going to wait with us?" "I will not go on alone brothers; I will be safer for all of us if I stay with you. We need to stay together."

"Of course, Seth" said Jervis, "we are not home yet so let us make a rest here and make a quick move across the Sibson fields to home".

The rain had started again, with a hailstorm and rumbles of thunder, all three men stepped inside the hovel, it was dark, dusty dirty but was dry and shelter from the approaching storm.

Thomas ventured up the rickety stairs and found two rooms, with a shuttered windows both rooms were small and dusty both had a bed, with a rough and dirty straw mattress badly infested with mice and the smell told Thomas, it was a lot of mice.!

There was little light coming in it was dark inside the cottage, the roof was leaking as the rain turned heavy. Thomas lay down on one of the straw beds, Jervis came up to see where Thomas was, Seth followed, "we might as well settle here for a while" said Thomas, "we can rest until the weather improves". "I agree" said Seth, "let us rest here". "Well brother it looks like you have found a comfortable pit to wallow"." It is not the best of beds said Thomas, but the mice have welcomed me".

The three men lay down and Jervis sat on a chair, the three men chatted foe while and talked about the terrible scenes they had witnessed that morning they listened to the rain rattling on the wooden roof, soon they were almost mesmerised by the sound of the rain and had rested until they were sleeping.

It was warm still, the rain was heavy, the storm lasted for an hour or more, Jervis was awakened by the sound of a dog barking in the distance, he lay there for a while reminding himself of the terrible day.

 As he lay there, he became aware of voices outside, he stood up sharply jarring his back, Jervis had always suffered with a complaining back, it was one of the troubles from being a blacksmith, heavy lifting and hard hammer work bought its toll, all the running through the wood earlier hadn't helped, he was of the mind the best thing was to get home secure the doors and windows and get some rest.

He crept slowly and went to the shuttered window, outside and below he could see two men, soldiers, wearing red scarves and leather caps and armour, horses were eating grass on the green opposite, he could not see any further than the end of the cottage.

He could hear three voices, he crept to the bed

side and put his hand across Thomas's mouth, Jervis held his finger to his lips, "Shussssh" he whispered, "bad men down below", Thomas opened his eyes and sat up, "be quite whispered" Jervis.

Jervis went across to Seth, he moved to Seth and did the same covering Seth's mouth, as Seth woke, he was startled and made a noise.

Jervis put his finger to his lips again, Seth eyes were wide open looking directly at Jervis. Jervis moved away and looked down on the men through the old broken floorboards, a shaft of light shine up through the floorboards, dust and airborne soil illuminated by the light from the door made for a vail between the gaze of Jervis and the strange men below.

The men downstairs were talking loudly, one of them was starting a fire in the fireplace, to dry their clothes, they had food and ale to hand, the weather had not improved, and if anything, the rain was getting worse.

Jervis whispered to Thomas and Seth that they must not move around, "we will have to wait until they have gone or sleeping before we make our escape", Thomas whispered we could jump from the window, no said Jervis that would make too much noise and alarm the men to their presence in the hovel. We have no weapons either said Seth.

The men down stairs were talking about the day on the field at Redemoor one was boasting of how he had heard the blood curdling cries of men he had cut down, running them through with his sword and cutting then across the neck with his halberd another said he had revelled in the hanging of a Yorkist he had caught on the run from the field , he boasted of the man's cries for his mother and children and his life as he sliced his ears off and stabbed him through the heart, " the bastard had nowhere to run,

"I slaught'r'd that bugger liketh the y'rkist pig that gent was!"

The three men laughed as they ate and munched on cold duck legs cuts of meat and roasted cold parsnips, they drank sour ale from a flagon taken from the field provisions kitchen on the back of Whitemoor, they spoke about returning home to Shrewsbury and the Welsh boarders.

Another was from Oswestry, he spoke of his land and his animals and his wife and 5 children waiting for his return with his battle wages to see them through the wintertime, he would also buy new horses and new sheep.

One man they called Idris started to sharpen his sword on the stone fireplace. Another said to him why are you doing that here your work with that blade has been done, this will be your last battle Idris, It will not be my last and I doubt your words Sir.

Maybe on this field today you rediscovered your bloodlust, only the bloodlust of killing the Englishman Idris replied, they madden me so, I wish the English well with a new King is also my wish, we today have lost good men and friends and battle cousins. The three men raised the flagon and cheered a toast "to god's love we send the brave, they will never be forgotten" each took a drink and continued to eat. Laughing and telling stories.

One of the men said solemnly I wish for my woman to be waiting for me when I return. Another said in a few days we will be back in our home. If I gallop with more speed than you then I could warm her up for you, you will die if you court her friendly ways. I will respond with a sharp knife and cut your cock off. The three men laughed and amidst odd chats about wives' brothers Shrewsbury, Nescliff and Oswestry getting home buying new land, horses, and clothes.

Jervis was hoping for the ale and full bellies would help see these three men off to a sleep and then Thomas Seth and Himself could slip out of the door undetected. It was soon clear the soldiers, tired after their day of killing and all the excitement of the rout, were drifting off to sleep, one had already head back had started snoring, one of the others kicked him to stop the noise, after short while and more arguments, leg pulling laughter and childish comments to each other soon all three were snoring.

After it had gone quiet for a while, Jervis whispered over to Thomas and Seth, let us see if we can get out, look, the door is clear, we just need to creep down and make a dash for it, no, said Thomas, there are three horses, if we take the horses they will not be able to follow us as we escape, good idea said Jervis, Seth said "I can't ride a horse", Jervis said "this will be a quick lesson then Seth. Let us check on the sleeping Tudors below."

Jervis led the way and opened the door, it creaked as he opened it, he stopped immediately, Thomas looked through the gap, he could see the three insurgents sleeping, mouths open, of foul breath and rotten teeth on show, discarded food scattered all around them, one of them farted and brushed a fly off his face.

"Now let us make our move," said Thomas.

Jervis opened the door enough they could make their way out of the upper rooms, Seth followed last, Thomas followed Jervis, the three men slowly made their way silently down the rickety stairs towards the door trying to step as lightly as they could across the worn floorboards towards the door, one of the soldiers belched, Jervis stopped and held a finger in the air.

The solider fidgeted in his settle, it was clear he was awake, Jervis and Thomas crouched down, Seth was on the bottom step of the stairs, he crouched down following Thomas's one-handed finger instruction to do the same.

The soldier stood up, Jervis' heart was beating so fast, he imagined that Thomas and Seth were the same but was too concentrated on the next move of the soldier to look around at his own brother.

The Soldier made his way staggering a few steps to the door, he stepped out of the hovel and in front of the door took a long and noisy piss.

He contained himself and looked left and right scratching his groin, then returned to his settle and made himself comfortable. In a couple of moments, he was asleep again, the three men were still like statues in the darkness at the back of the room.

Thomas had almost fainted from the stress and

stench of these dirty strange insurgents, Jervis made a tentative step, as he did, another soldier moved the three men stopped again, holding their breaths, the soldier turned in his seat.

Jervis looked back at the other two, and beckoned Thomas and Seth to follow him step by step. they tipped toed across the floor the soldiers only a few feet away. Jervis made it through the door, Thomas followed quickly after, Seth came through last, as he did, he looked and saw a sword stood up against the fireplace, it was in his reach, he stopped in the doorway and put his hand out toward the sword, just as he did the soldier closest his hand dropped in his relaxed slumber to his side and caught Seth's sleeve pushing Seth's hand to the side.

Seth was startled and pulled his hand away as he did the solider stirred, Seth made a leap for the door, his shoulder banging against the doorframe, it banged hard, as he got outside, Jervis and Thomas were leading two of the three horses into the thicket behind the cottage, Seth came running round the corner, one of them is coming he said, Jervis Immediately said "Shush "and waved his hands down gesture!

"Come let us go", Seth called as he ran for all his life, Jervis had mounted the first horse, Thomas was running the other down the drover's lane running back down toward the back road, Seth was running behind Thomas, running close behind Seth was a soldier he was a big man, he had a good gait on him and was catching up on Seth fast. Come back here shouted the soldier.

Thomas turned and saw the burly sight behind, he called forward to Jervis, Jervis pulled back and slowed the horse down, he turned and saw Seth's predicament.

Jervis called to Thomas to make a move away with Seth, and quickly, Jervis rode the horse directly at the solider, the soldier stopped and stood to one side of the drover's lane.

Jervis swerved the horses back end into the soldier, in one move the horses rear legs trampled down on the solider, he cried out to his comrades, over the hedges Jervis could see the other two soldiers making their way over towards the commotion.

Jervis swiped his reins at the horse's rump, she took off towards Seth and Thomas who was now mounted on the second horse, Seth had run ahead and was a good distance down the drover's lane. Thomas caught him up and pulled Seth onto the rear of the horse, "Seth, hold on tight", Thomas called to his passenger, seeing Jervis returning dug his heels in hard and galloped off away from the approaching soldiers, Jervis followed close behind, they rode hard and fast Seth holding on for his dear life.

After a good time, Jervis stopped and looked back across the fields, they have galloped to Ratcliffe close to Sheepy Magna a village not far off, in no time and made good distance from the attackers.

CHAPTER 16

Soon they came upon a young man in a lane quite near to Sheepy, Thomas said to him, "good day I am Thomas from Carltonstone, this is my friend Seth from Carltonstone, and behind us is my brother Jervis, we need to hide these horses what is your name boy" Thomas asked, "Good day to you sirs, I am Richard Barkeley" replied to the man, he removed his hat and bowed his head, "can you offer us direction and some water", "I can", said the young man. "But are you honourable men?", he smiled, "We are good men" replied Thomas "we are being pursued by three foreign soldiers from the Welsh boarders who have been murderous in a battle over Redemoor this very day."

"These horses are not local stock are they", "they are not" said Jervis Thomas said, "you are knowledgeable Sir", I am a seller of such beasts, if you can offer us direction to Smisby or Carltonstone these beasts can be yours for the selling".

There are vagabond soldiers in chase of us, so we need to hide or make our escape on foot. Richard Barkeley said, "I can help you; I have a hayrick to deliver to my uncle at Wellsborough this very afternoon, I can hide you in my cart and we can make escape for you."

"That Sir would be very welcome can we do this now, I fear we could be discovered soonest".

"Let me lead you to some water, then we can make our way" Richard Barkeley said.

The horses were taken to the rear of the manor house and placed in a stable, Richard Barkeley took all the saddles and harnesses off the horses and placed them in a field and paddock with other mares to the southern side of the manor house, he gave instructions to another man there to guard the horses and if foreign men came by to lead them away from these beasts.

The three men took water from a stream and were feeling much better, Richard Barkeley came into the lane with the hayrick and three cuts of a bread loaf and some apples, "eat these you look as if you need sustenance, we are thankful Richard Barkeley, you are welcome replied Richard as he moved the hayrick cart forward, "come let us be on our way."

The four men rode on the cart, a single broad backed horse trotted gently pulling them along the lanes towards Wellsboro, "can't we go faster"? asked Thomas impatiently, he was keeping a good look out for soldiers coming their direction, which thankfully there was not.

"No said Richard Barkeley if we go faster, we may bring attention to this cart and our quest will be fruitless", "I agree" said Jervis "it is not too far". "If you need to hide, go under the front of the haystack on the middle here, I have a covering here, I can make a hiding for you under that".

After a good distance Jervis said, "that was a fine manor house you work at Richard", "I don't work there said Richard, "so what were you doing there?", "It is my home, I live there with my father and my mother, he is also known as Richard Barkeley.

I see are you a noble man asked Thomas, not really, he said, we just own some land there and in Ashby, so what is your work asked Seth, I buy and Sell beasts, we as a family breed, horses and bovine for sale at the markets in Twycross and Redemoor and Measham.

You have done well for your family asked Jervis, yes, we have done honourable and good business for many years. That is good, I am impressed, and you sir what is your trade, we are wheelwrights and blacksmiths, and Seth is the toll keeper from our village.

You may be good men to acquaint said Richard we need carts rebuilding and new wheels fitting many times. Thomas said we are welcome to meet with you Richard we can perhaps work for each other. I think that would be worthy said Richard Barkeley.

The four men continued and as they crossed the Burton Road they started to climb up to Wellsboro and the settlement there, the Hayrick was burdened with a heavy load and the horse was slowing down as they climbed the last few yards, Jervis and Thomas slipped off the Hayrick cart, there at the top there were two men dressed in smocks and waiting,

Good day to you Richard said one of them, we have been watching your approach, I see you have help today, well yes we have help today, this is Jervis And Seth and Thomas, I know Jervis said Richard uncle, you are from Carlton-stone, I am acquainted with you yes said Jervis, I have made you a scythe for your meadow cuttings, you did and good tools they are Jervis, it is good to see you. And you sir said Jervis, the other man was called Mathew, he was a broad man, his head was bald, and he had bushy eyebrows and big ears.

Thomas bid him good day. Mathew said to Jervis, have you three been in trouble today? Before Jervis or Thomas could answer he asked again, are you three running from the square battle this day, we are witnesses to the battle, we were caught up in the run from the battle field and have been chased by soldier's, we managed to escape and made a run for home but we have been ....Never mind that now, take off your shirts, What? said Jervis , "Take off your shirts" Mathew repeated, "for what purpose?" Thomas asked, "there are four soldiers making for here right now look, Mathew pointed to the Burton Road below, "now take your shirts off and do it now". the three men Jervis Thomas and Seth did as they were told, each man was given a wooden hay fork and told to follow the hayrick and unload it by hand. They complied;

Matthew hid the dirty shirts in a nearby empty barrel.

Mathew closed the gate behind him and walked to the yard where the hayrick was being unloaded. "You there" shouted a soldier from the lane, "you stop there - come here", Mathew stopped and looked back, Can I help you men? he enquired. "Who are those men there, Mathew looked around to where Seth and Thomas were lifting the stacks of hay from the back of the cart, those men? Mathew pointed at Jervis and Thomas, yes said the soldier, these are my workers helping with the harvest, why? What are their names, Mathew said Jervis Thomas and Seth, why? Have any of you been witnesses to ta fight not 2 miles from here this morning, Mathew came right alongside the soldier's horse and said "What fight? I know not of any hurley burley this day. Well good for your own men and women said Mathew, We are simple land and feld workers Sire we have no intention for fighting. Have these men in your employ been here all day, well for most of the day said Mathew, they fetch and carry the hay on the hayrick cart from here to Sheepy, some 2 miles to the East, so not of any other place have they been today Sire.

Very well then said the soldier make about your business and be off with you. "Good day to you sire said Mathew as he made his way across the yard to the men working hard to clear the cart. The soldiers moved off and continued back along Burton Road.

" Thank you, Mathew," said Richard Barkely "have they gone"? they have moved on but slowly, so be careful Jervis. Mathew cautioned, make your way back to Carltonstone across the field there yonder Mathew pointed and nodded his head. If you look from here, you can see down to Carlton there where the smoke trail is coming from.

They made their way back towards Redemoor and made their way along the backs of the village walking quickly.

The Redemoor market square was full of Tudor Soldiers, the market square was crowded with horses and riders, singing and celebrations were in full sway.

Jervis, Thomas, and Seth passed through the back lane and within a quarter of a mile onto the field at the back of Carltonstone there they could see the smoke rising through the low clouds over towards Carltonstone. "

Look said Seth, there is fire in the village", "I see that said Jervis, come let us approach this side of the river", it took a long while to get to the back of the village, the back field was a gentle slope up to the main track and the edge of the river, there they moved slowly in and out of the tree long the river bank, across they could see into the village, Jervis led them through the spinney at the back of Sharps perch next to the church.

From this vantage point they saw several men in the village on horses, these were not local men, Jervis crouched down low.

Thomas sidled besides him, who are they he asked, how do I know? snapped Jervis, that fire is from my yard. Thomas and Seth continued to watch for a while, these men were either drunk or on a rampage.

Jervis decided he needed a closer look, they crossed the stream there across a fallen tree, the three men stooped low out of sight as they approached the rear of Thomas' s cottage moving slowly through Coopers Perch.

Thomas Seth and Jervis made it into Thomas's cottage it has been ransacked the place was a trashed home, pots and goblets strewn across the small rooms, the doors were knocked away from their hinges and the floor covered in food and bed clothes. Thomas made his way upstairs, there from the crack in the shutters he could see Soldiers in the yard opposite.

They were burning Jervis's things, tools and clothes; 3 men were drinking ale from their beer flagon filled the day before. They were celebrating, rowdy and drunk.

Jervis came to Thomas, what can you see he asked? They are making a fire Jervis, let me see shouted Jervis, one of the men in the Yard heard Jervis 's voice and called another soldier, they came across and made their way into the cottage,

Immediately Seth was set upon, Jervis shouted down to leave him alone, they dragged Seth out into the wet lane, Seth was knocked to the ground and a pike held to his throat, who are you? said one of the soldiers, Im just a villain said Seth I live at the top of the lane where do you live villain? Shouted one of the men, I live in the toll house, he replied shaking with fear. So, you will be a rich man? One of the soldiers pulled Seth up and kicked him in the buttocks, come let us see your coins villain.

Jervis burst out from the cottage, this is my yard, and I am the blacksmith here, you men be on your way. Four soldiers approached Jervis, "so this is your yard"?, it is said Jervis and that is my ale which you are welcome to, but for all this defacement, there is no thanks, now be on your way.

Six men came to see Jervis, they were young soldiers, full of ale and high spirits, in their late teens and early 20's young inexperienced but pushing their luck with Jervis. He called to them" be on your way", they started to laugh, "be on your way men", or what? one of them called, "or the lord will strike you down" came another voice from across the lane, there stood Peter the Priest in his long robes and stick he said, "enough ruffians if you value your futures leave now". the rabble of drunken youngsters laughed; the rain was now getting heavy.

Peter called to Seth, "Seth come hither to me" the Soldier holding Seth let go of Seth's coat, Seth walked beside the priest, they both walked to Jervis and Thomas, the four men walked toward the soldiers, The priest saying, "go men it's time for you to leave, go away now, go, do your duty".

"There will be a new King, he is your sovereign now go and do your duties." Four of the soldiers mounted their horse close by, two were on foot. Approached Jervis their swords drawn Jervis stood firm, get away Jervis growled this is not your land, so go away and join your army in Redemoor where you belong, the two men came close to Jervis, they took a threatening stance.

Jervis moved forward, to face the men, the two young men were called by the others on horseback, they backed away and ran up the lane to catch them up getting a lift on the back of the horses as they left.

Jervis went to the yard the fire was raging, Thomas went to the well and bought two pales of water he threw them on the fire and put out the main part of the flames, more shouted Jervis, I want it out completely.

Seth and Thomas fetched and carried many buckets of water the rain started again it came down heavy and helped and eventually put the fire out, the smoke and steam were hanging in the wet air, the lane was littered in possessions taken in their rampage. One or two the villagers were starting to re appear after hiding in the woods and some walking back from Barton and Bufton Lodge.

Thomas and Jervis had returned to their homes and started to clear up the damage and mess, Jervis left the yard to cool down, he wanted to secure his home and get his possessions together and in hand. The mess was everywhere, the cottage had been trashed and ransacked Thomas was seeing a similar disaster in his home.

CHAPTER 17

The two brothers met up in the smithy yard some short time later. Thomas was still stinking in his blood infused clothes and according to Jervis and Seth it wasn't getting any better, Jervis said you need to wash the stench from yourself brother you are giving off a foul odour. Thomas took no notice he ignored the comments, he had many questions as to what they should do next. "What shall we do about our families Jervis," "I'm not sure if it is safe to see them back home, look at the top of the village, there are still soldiers passing through these parts. Thomas was anxious, Jervis tried to calm him, "We risk too much, those are my words Thomas, but I hear your concern".

Jervis scratched his head; he was still covered in soot and dirty and wishing himself he could have a bathe. The late afternoon into early evening had turned hot and sticky, the air was still and uncomforting, the sky was threatening rain and perhaps a fierce storm. Jervis continued, "We need to keep out of sight or be prepared to protect ourselves, I consider we may have to fight for our liberty, there was news of bands and squads of soldiers were going house to house looking for "routers" this gave Jervis great concern for their safety.

Thomas was deep in thought, he turned to Jervis, "Brother, I respect what you say, I want to take a horse back to Smisby and bring the wives and children back home", Jervis shook his head, "this is not advised Thomas" said Jervis, there is still too many men being chased down, we could come across the mercenaries of the battle on our ways, they could strike us down with no reason, then what will Anna and Clara have? It will be better Thomas if we wait here till morning".

"Come with me" said Jervis, he placed what was left of the gates to the yard together, "come" he further continued to encourage Thomas out of his maudlin ways, "we need to sort you out!" said Jervis, "what is so important other than our family?

"Nothing is more important than making you smell like a king; your bodily dis-ease is offensive to my nose!"

"Thomas smiled, that's better said Jervis come we will go and bathe in the Meash. We shall find something to eat, I have a ferdekyn of ale and some morsels for your comfort. Go find a fresher shirt and pants, I will call on you shortly."

Thomas made his way across to his home, inside his belongings were scattered as the rampaging soldiers had trashed the house with no respect, Thomas thought it was a good thing that Anna and the children has fled to Smisby, his tears made it clear he was desperate to see they were safe.

He found a pair of pants and a fresh shirt, and bought them with him to meet Jervis outside, they walked the few hundred yards to the river, below the village, it was in fast flow with all the rain of the previous days, it was brown and fast flowing but to the two dirty brothers it looked refreshing and inviting, they soon had de-robed and threw themselves in to the well-known bathing hollow.

The water was indeed a welcome fresh bathe Jervis handed Thomas a patty of soap made from tallow, ashes, and lye, they washed each other's backs and rinsed in the flowing waters. The two brothers also washed off their clothes covered in blood and the detritus of the warring day they had endured.

Thomas said, "that feels much better brother, it was a welcome dip", "Yes, I agree with that brother you are smelling much more like the King than before" said Jervis, "now let us dry off and get to work in preparing for the return of the loved ones". "Indeed", said Thomas.

They cleaned their boots and dressed making their way up to the Village in better spirits than before.

In the yard was Peter the priest, "Ah Jervis" he said as the two brothers approached. "Yes, Peter what is it? "There is a bloodied fighting man in my lodgings, he has called for me to ask if you are safe, I think he is Richard Sharnford, but he is in a bad ways he is injured and needs prayers, can you come." "I will, said Jervis, Jervis dropped his clothes off in the yard and made his way to Peters Lodgings next to the Chapel, inside was Richard Sharnford, he was blooded and breathing heavily.

He looked at Jervis, he moved his weight from one side to the other to get a better view of Jervis and Thomas, he groaned as he moved his arm, he let out a cry as it was agonising him the pain in his shoulder was sharp and acute, he said "you are safe Blacksmith", "I am and thanks to you Richard", Richard and Jervis clasped hands. "My dear friend" said Jervis "What have you done?"

Thomas looked on from the edge of the tiny room. Jervis looked over Richard, he had a deep wound on his upper left arm it was raw and bleeding, his ribs were cut, bruised and painful it was clear he had taken a blow from something sharp and heavy probably on his horse and at a gallop.

It was starting to get dark, the light to see in the small room was dim and not good.

Jervis said to "Thomas, go and get me the pot of mustard, salt, some honey and bring me some fresh muslin and a handful of mint leaves", Thomas said nothing but bolted off to collect the things Jervis had requested.

Jervis pulled back Richard Sharnford's jerkin and shirt to reveal a deep wound, probably from a broad sword swipe, it was down to the shoulder bone, causing Richard extremes of acute pains as he tried to move into a comfortable position he screamed out as he postured.

Jervis looked at Peter, he whispered this will need to be closed, there was a lot of blood, but the raw meat of Richard Sharnford shoulder was on display and would if not closed would fester and a miserable death would occur".

Jervis pulled Peter away from Richard Sharnford so he could whisper to him, "this man needs to be closed of his wounds, do you have notice of a physician", "no Jervis I do not, the nearest man of practise is at Leicester or over to Coven tree, so some time away, by which he could die of his injury". "I see said Jervis our hope is all we may have for my friend".

Peter stood by muttering a prayer in Latin and threading his beads furiously through his hands and arthritic fingers.

Thomas arrived back with a muslin cloth and mustard seeds honey and mint, Jervis made small pockets of cloth filled with salt, crushed Mustard seed and mint leaves infused with honey, he cleaned the wound with water Peter had blessed the poultices and placed them on and around Richard Sharnford's lesser cuts and wounds, Richard! Jervis called to him, "these poultices will make to a fever which will not harm you and will heal your marks."

"I do not have knowledge of the wound on his shoulder other than with horses and beasts who have fallen, but this is a man and I know not of his disorder or how we can prevent him dying, we will make him comfortable here and see his wound in the morning".

Richard Sharnford was still breathing hard, the pain from his broken and cracked ribs was considerable and he was troubled in his catching of his breath.

Jervis pleaded with Richard Sharnford to try and relax and let the anx't go, "think about your breathing, and try to rest your head".

Jervis offered Richard Sharnford a drink from a small wooden bowl he raised his head, so he did not choke on the tepid drink.

Jervis placed Richard's head on the pillow gently and told him to rest, "come hither Peter and you Thomas, we must talk"

The three men walked outside, the rain was coming down heavily and the track outside the chapel was turning to a mire again.

Jervis said "I can see from his shoulder wound he has a chance to contract a rotting of his flesh, I have not used the hot iron on a fellow man, you know this", I do said Peter," but what do we do? - do nothing and he could die, do something and take the better chance he will live, only then would we have a clear consciences if the worst was to come to us."

"I cannot see this man suffer, he saved my life, our lives today Thomas", "yes he did brother, and we owe him that chance in return".

"He will become terribly ill and soonest, the rotting of the flesh will take hold and he will suffer the worst of poisoning and prolonged misery."

Jervis held silent for a while, deep in thought he spoke to Thomas and Peter, "It might be good for Richard if we attack his wounds tonight so that he can sleep and he rests well, his recovery can be prayed for, and he will enjoy the morning again. Thomas said, "we will do what is right Jervis and we follow your words".

"Jervis, you have my blessing to try to save this man, it will be a hard task for a friend but with the good lord behind you and im sure Richard Sharnford's plea to save himself." Jervis and Thomas looked unsure where to start "Act now Jervis, I will follow you," said Peter.

Jervis looked to his brother for moral support, "Jervis you can and are the only man that can do this, what do we need."?

Jervis said to Peter "can we use your room to carry out this, yes of course" said Peter "I will fetch clean cloths and water, we need to heat the water too, so light a good fire"! "I will attend to that" said Peter and off he set to find the list of items.

Come with me said Jervis to Thomas, we need to find some knives, Irons, and pokes in the forge yard.

"Jervis you must not fear, today this time, you have used your wisdom and defiance of fear to do an honourable thing".

Jervis was troubled by the notion of treating a man with the hot iron to resolve his wounds, but he knew also this was the only choice.

"Right Thomas we need two more men, go and find Seth and Phillip they are big men. Bring silk thread, Anna will have some in her sewing basket. And we will find the irons and blades from the yard."

Peter, I want you to bathe his wounds and removed his leather jerkin, Peter lit candles in the room so there was a better light as the night was darkening even more, he removed Richard's shirt and, Richard was starting to shiver, a sign fever may be setting in.

Peter dowsed his head with cool water. "I pray

for you son" said Peter Richard eyes were darting left and right, he was mumbling something, rolling his head from side to side like he was demented, Peter hoped the brothers would not be long and this could be over.

Thomas was the first to arrive back with Seth and Phillip, Jervis came soon after. Jervis cleaned a dagger and short sword. I know not which the best is to be used. Thomas looked at the deep gash in Richard's shoulder, it was as long as a man's hand span and had opened up to be two fingers wide and was deep perhaps to the bone below.

Thomas said to Jervis "the dagger will not hold enough heat Jervis, the sword is better", Jervis said "aye lad I know", Jervis pushed the sword into the fire grate the room was now stifling hot, Seth and Phillip came into the room.

"Now then everyone "Jervis looked at all the men with a bowed head, "I need you to hold this man down, I am going to hurt him, when I do he will try to get up, maybe even fight, he is, as you witness see he is a big strong man I need him still, So Thomas you will hold his arms down with Phillip, Seth you and Peter will sit on his legs",

"I will do the work then hold him down, you will need all your might and a strong stomach, this will not be pleasant."

Jervis washed his hands, he whispered to Richard drink this brandy, he held out a goblet of sour brandy it was the strongest drink available, Richard Sharnford sat up a little and drank it down in one! Jervis raised his eyebrows, forgive me Richard Sharnford." Jervis hands were shaking, and he was sweating in the heat of the small room.

Richard looked at him, his eyes were not focussing on Jervis he was almost delirious with the fever and the boozy drink he had just consumed. Jervis swung around and came back with a huge well aimed punch, which caught Richard on the jawbone just below his ear, Richard slumped back onto the table unconscious.

Jervis said to Thomas and Seth get ready, Seth Phillip and Thomas with Peter took u their positions, Jervis turned over the sword tip in the fire, the end wasn't red hot, Jervis positioned Seth lower down on Richard's legs, he instructed Thomas to open up the wound, placing his hands on one side of the gash and pulling it open, the wound was weeping with blood and puss and was starting to smell unpleasant, Jervis checked the fire again, he withdrew the sword from the fire the tip was orange hot, Jervis wiped it with a piece of leather, the hiss of the blade was clear in the room and a smell of burnt leather filled the air.

He pushed in back into the hearth, each man was hot and nervous, each man waited silently as Richard Sharnford was starting to writhe beneath them.

The time is now said Jervis suddenly, Thomas held the shoulder open, Thomas pulled on the shoulder wound and Richard Sharnford called out, Jervis pulled the sword from the fire pit, he wiped the end again and the air was infused with the smell of burning, Jervis called to the other men to hold Richard down and hold him hard with all your might.

Jervis said quietly men now, he bought the sword close to the wound and placed it into the slash and drew it slowly along the wound, touching the raw flesh on each side. Richard Sharnford arched his back and gave out a long guttural scream, "Hold him down called out Jervis, Jervis looked at the wound it was smoking, Richard was still arching his back and screaming, Jervis placed the sword back into the fireplace.

Peter said "Jervis! My god man not more.?" "Yes, more said Jervis, Richard had lain back down on the bed, Jervis was watching Richard closely, "forgive me I see your pain Richard, but I need to make another pass".

The fire was starting to spit as the sword was again orange hot. Richard was looking at Jervis, his eyes were wide with fear, no! no! no! called out Richard, his body was shaking, and he was spitting and foaming at the mouth no! no! no! he screamed.

Jervis said to the others, hold him down tight with all your might, the four big men held and pushed Richard tight down Into the bed.

"Again", Jervis called to Thomas to hold the wound open, he reached for the sword he held it high, Richard saw the weapon with a red-hot tip moving toward him he drew in a lung full of breath, Nooo! Nooo! Richard Sharnford screamed from the bottom of his soul; Jervis shouted hold - him – down!

Jervis placed the red-hot tip of the sword at the top of the gash, the smell of burning flesh filled the room the wound hissed and seared the flesh as it was covered with the red-hot sword.

Thomas was baulking with the smell just a short distance from his face, Peter was convulsing trying not to vomit as the smell of the burning skin.

Richard Sharnford was screaming, his body was contorted and trying desperately to escape the source of this hideous pain his screams turned to squeals, the four men holding him down were troubled by the spectacle, Seth and Phillip almost ready to run away, like a scolded pig Richard conveyed vocally his acute sharp piercing agony, Jervis held the sword on the side of the wound for a short while making sure he cleared the puss away.

Richard Sharnford dropped on the bed the pain had overcome his senses and his resolve, he passed out and his body slumped and relaxed into the bed.

Now we must work quickly to close up the gashed wound, Jervis threw the sword to the ground, he looked haggard, and a terse look was about his face, this was troubling and sickening to Jervis and would have been if it was an animal, but to a fellow man this was even worse.

Jervis took the silk thread from Thomas, he threaded it through a long needle, he made a first attempt to get it through the skin close to the wound, it was tough and not as easy as Jervis had thought or hoped for his needles were more used on leather and canvas, less the skin of a friend suffering trauma at his own hands.

After a few passes, the wound was starting to close, Richard was still out cold, and on the bed the four men surrounding the bed were in awe of Jervis, as he worked without talking, his head sweating working hard to close up the huge gash in Richard Sharnford's shoulder.

Stitch by stitch the wound was closed, Richard Sharnford was starting to look a little more normal. Jervis asked that the men leave the room and join them at the forge.

They moved out of the room, Peter poured water on the fire and opened the shutters, the cool of the evening came through and the rain outside was cooling the room down and taking the unpleasant stench of burning flesh away.

Jervis finished off with a tight knot, Richard Sharnford was sleeping, he was peaceful and quiet as he slept.

Peter said, "are you done now Jervis?", "I am now Peter he is done; we shall see if the fever breaks and he settles down, Surely, he will Peter replied.

Peter took Jervis firmly by the arm and said,

"With the hot iron of holy fear to prevent the festering of some other disorder; and keep the places you have cauterized warm with the fire of charity and the oil of mercy that they may not be chilled by the touch of impiety. …Jervis, this is your friend and as so, you will then take the virtues of humility, patience and obedience, and mix them with the honey of the divine word, and carefully store this remedy in the cupboard of your mind, you have tried to save this man with goodness and kindness I am sure of it".

"Now let me continue to watch him, I will spare a vigil for him this night and keep him in god's care."

Jervis bowed his head and said thank you to Peter.

Jervis collected his implements and made off toward the yard, taking a swipe at Peters bottle of brandy as he left the room. The cool air outside was fresh and welcome. Peter covered Richard Sharnford and settled down for the night.

CHAPTER 18

There waiting for Jervis was Thomas Seth and Phillip, Thomas handed Jervis a drink of beer from the firkin Jervis had hidden, Jervis drank with gusto from the wooden pint pot, spilling it down his chin and neck as he gulped it down, it was good, Jervis drank it down in one sitting.

Another brother? Asked Thomas, yes another, that was the worst thing I have ever done!" "No" said Seth "that was the bravest thing I have ever seen Jervis". Jervis replied with "what could I have done?" holding his hands out, all three men patted Jervis on the back, Jervis looked back towards Peters house a look of dread was on his face, he was regretful of the pain he caused his friend. He slightly said a prayer.

Thomas came across to Jervis, "come on brother let us rest now". "Yes" Jervis said snapping himself out of his doubts, "I'm with hunger and need a morsel to eat, bread was passed around stale and hard crusted, but welcome with some curds and honey it made good eating and comforting as it was swilled down with more ale.

Later, Seth and Phillip said their good nights, they made their ways home well-oiled with ale and in shock at what was before then only a short time before.

Jervis and Thomas settled down in the yard and drank ale, until brothers both were sleeping with full bellies and a sated comfortable feeling under the cover of the yards lean too. Both their minds unfettered by the events of the long, long day.

Throughout the night men were heard scuttering through the village in the middle of the night through the mud and mire still on the ground after the weeks of rain and wet.

Soldiers came too, marching through, men on horseback making their way back to Nottingham and Leicester.

Carltonstone was a backwater, "a rat run" as Jervis called it. It remained off the beaten track and although the village was prosperous it did it so in a quiet unannounced way.

Dawn broke late the next day, the clouds were low on the horizon blocking any cheer from a low easterly sunrise. Jervis was awake first, his shoulders aching from his arthritic joints, there was a slight wind as he rose from his hard uncomfortable cold wet yard bed down.

He stood up slowly and stretched out his arms and bent his back over to rid himself of the beer infused slumber, after a long and loud yawn, he glanced down a Thomas, he was wrapped up in his old clothes, his one boot was on the wrong foot he was sleeping deeply, laying their mouth open dreaming, and snoring like a piglet.

Jervis went to the well and drew up some water, he poured it over his head was washed himself down, he took a couple of sips from his hands as he scooped up hands full of refreshing cool water.

He looked across the lane at his cottage, it was quiet and still, it wasn't its normal happy hovel, with no noise from the children as they played,

Jervis knew he would have the clean it up before Clara returned, his mind soon came to thinking about her and the boy, and how stupid he had been in going to the witness the battle yesterday, what an idiot he thought to himself.

And for Thomas too he felt responsible, if bad things had of happened, Thomas may have not returned to be the good father he himself, was proud to call his little brother.

Jervis heard footsteps approaching, it was Peter, he looked tired and weary, "Good Morning Peter said Jervis, you look tired" , "I have not slept much said Peter, praying for the sick and wounded is a hard task and the lord will issue no rest until they are safe".

"How is Richard Sharnford, this morning"? Enquired Jervis, "He is sleeping Jervis, and there seems to be no fever. His wound is still angry, and he has moved and woken with its pains." "I Will call on him in a while, we have some clearing up to do after the events of yesterday," said Jervis. "Indeed, you do Jervis, where is your brother?" "He is sleeping too; it is still too early for his awakening". "Not so" said Peter "here he comes, Thomas approached looking dirty and not too well, Jervis my head hurts", "I should think it will do Brother you drank the last of the ale!" Peter said, "at some time today can you find some food for Richard Horse, I have given it some water, but it needs to graze", Thomas said we will feed the horse and it needs some exercise too? "Does it said Jervis, yes said Thomas "it will need to be ridden at least to Smisby", "Smisby replied Peter "ah I know Thomas I Know". Thomas had a big grin on his face and was looking at Jervis for approval.

Jervis said we will wait until the homes are cleared of the damage, then we shall plan to get the family back here. Peter said it should be fine now the numbers of fighting men has lessened.

"So, Thomas go to your home and do what is needed, I will brother said Thomas", he set off toward his small cottage next to Jervis's cottage.

"Peter I will come with you to see Richard Sharnford". "I will come to him later said Peter, there had been a report of trouble up at the toll house, when I have finished my business there, I will return to oversee Richard Sharnford again". Jervis said, "I will not stay long Peter."

Jervis went across to Peters small cottage next to the chapel, inside he found Richard sitting up sipping a drink of water. "Good morning Jervis said, "Richard nodded his head" "how are you this morning"," I am alive said Richard, in pain but alive, Jervis looked under the dressing on Richard's shoulder, it was clean and tight, although Richard looked pale and tired.

"I will suggest to you Richard that you stay here for a few days to recover, we will bring some food for you when you feel like eating", "I thank you again Jervis, croaked Richard.

"I am sorry to have returned here to put you to all this trouble". Richard said, "It is a good job you did come here; you may not have survived the wounding replied Jervis.

"It was my fault, and I am to blame, I was attending to the business of the King when he was reported killed, I went to rescue you and some others locally, I was ambushed by some unknowing French soldiers, they engaged me in a fight."

"I naturally fought back and hard, but had a sword swiped at me from a French mercenary savage, he caught me and pulled me off my horse and hence he had the upper hand and cut me. I managed to scramble back on my ride, she bought me here."

"You are fortunate Richard the wound was deep and albeit long, it was clean, I have used the hot iron to rid you of the infection, your other slashes have been treated with poultices of honey and herbs, they should heal in time". "You are a man of many talents said Richard, a blacksmith, a cart repairman and a physician", "no, no said Jervis, it takes a resolve only the lord can bestow to attend to wounds like this. And we all worked together last night", "I am obliged Jervis said Richard with a groan".

"I am asking for a favour in a way", "ask away then Jervis" said Richard, "I need Thomas to go to Smisby to call back our families, yes of course said Richard, of course" "Jervis, use my horse, send Thomas. Jervis smiled and thanked Richard.

Jervis left the cottage just as Reverend Peter had returned, "is it all well at the toll house? Yes, it is now but we have lost another villager to this swett disease.

"The wife of the toll hose keeper Seth was unwell with his return late last night; she expired this morning. Another soul lost this weekend" said Peter, "Poor Seth, he had a long day with us yesterday, Jervis replied "Indeed" said Peter "I'm sure he didn't expect to lose Catherine, no he is angry and unsettled by the loss of such a fine lady". "She was that," said Jervis.

"Oh, Jervis said Peter "there will be no service this morning, I will hold a service for all this evening", "I will pass the word around" said Jervis, thank you Jervis, I think we all need some time to reflect on the happenings of the last day and night."

"I will see you later", Peter passed by Jervis to enter his cottage, Peter bolted the door behind him, Jervis made his was across the lane to the yard, there he found Thomas clearing the burnt ashes from the yard, "Thomas, I have the permission of Richard to use his horse, you can use it to go to Smisby, if the lanes are clear you could go the green lane way and bring back the cart and Bessy. "

"Good" said Thomas," I will make my way shortly, Jervis our well is full of rubbish, it need clearing", "I will attend to that said Jervis, you get away with the horse and we will see you here later." "Water the horse and take a bag with you, keep off all main tracks, the soldiers will still be about, be fox like in your progress", "Stop worrying brother", "I'm not worried about you" Jervis said, I'm worried about Clara and Anna and the children.

CHAPTER 19

So, leave those sweepings and go now" said Jervis, "I am on my way said Thomas excitedly. Thomas took Richard's horse to the river, he washed it down removing blood and mud from its flanks.

Thomas led the horse back to the back of his own cottage and saddled it with his own saddle, he removed the battle garb and reins. Thomas mounted the horse, it was skittish at first but soon settled down, he rode past the yard wishing Jervis a good day.

Soon Thomas was galloping along the country back waters, he felt confident, and the horse was moving well, he could see over the hedges and was keeping his eyes out for soldiers and any military men who might be making their own way, it was still dull overhead and he passed through several showers of rain, he passed one or two people making their own way here and there.

He thought he might be a morning's ride to Smisby passing through the villages and hamlets of Measham and Sweep stone, Heather, and Raven stone. As he approached Ashby via Packington sometime later, he took a resting, he drank and let the horse drink from a small stream. The horse was steaming in the rain, Thomas looked on and wished he could have mare like this one.

On the horizon he could see a military encampment many tents and mounted soldiers were in view. He thought for a while as to the best way into Smisby without meeting Military men, he knew they would be unsympathetic to his plight, it was a Sunday a day of rest and worship, he knew he would have to be careful.

Smisby is placed on the northern side of Ashby, he could see Ashby castle close to the busy encampment. He decided to make for Newbold near Coleorton, there he could track across the drover's lanes to his cousin's village of Smisby.

Back In Carltonstone Jervis was making good progress on tidying the cottage and clearing the yard, no damage was done in the yard, and although the fire was set by the drunk soldiers it caused more mess that damage, Jervis lit a new fire in the forge pit and made good his tools to start working on a scythe for a farmer in Barlstone.

Peter came to him asking if Thomas had gone to Smisby.

"He has gone and should be with Clara and Anna any time now. I don't expect him back before evening as there will be the children to make safe on the cart" "of course, the Children, I see you will be relieved on their safe return" said Peter, "Yes indeed it has been a dramatic few days". "We will look forward to seeing the place get back to normal".

I will not stop you from your work remember the service is later this evening, we will give thanks for our families and being safe from harm. "Yes", replied Jervis, "we will be there".

Peter made his way to the back of the Chapel,

his robes wet at the foot and his hands covering his head as the rain came again.

Jervis worked hard to keep the fire alight. He would here the rattle of the Aleman's cart as it approached. Do you have any empty flagons he called across, I have broken one's said Jervis, we had drunken soldiers in the village last night and some were broken, I need as many as I can said the Aleman, he dropped off fresh ale to Jervis chatting as he did so.

"I hear there has been a battle nearby and see the wreckage left in the marketplace in Redemoor, men were chased from the village, and they disperse back to Ann Beame hill on this morning."

"The aldermen have promised fines and charges, the aldermen also said dead bodies are being buried on the battlefield in their 100's ws there that many killed Jervis?",

 "I can vouch as a witness there were many killed In the fighting" said Jervis "it was a bad day for the Yorkist king," "really?" said the Aleman, "yes said Jervis he was killed not more than a fields distance from where Thomas and I were watching."

"Did you see it"? "yes, we saw the French soldiers surround him and murder him like a wild animal, never before have I see such a brutalisation of a man let alone a fighting king."

"Yet yonder and before us were many men who lost their lives', and I would say there will be more deaths discovered in the coming days as they fell and were cut down to be left in the rivers and lanes around this place".

"Many men ran for their lives and me and Thomas were caught up in the fleeing from that murderous place."

"We had a long day getting back to Carlton-stone". The Aleman had a troubled look on his face, "we have never had this horror in these parts, Jervis, why here"? He enquired of Jervis, "I have no idea said Jervis, it was a meeting of armies, and someone had to lose, it was the first to fall would take the loss, it looks like the King had taken the worst of conclusions."

"My lord", said the Aleman "we should be thankful for god's kind mercy and that we can still talk to each other today". "I agree," said Jervis.

Peter arrived back and called to the Aleman," I am pleased you are here; I need a flagon of your best ale for an injured man in my cottage, can you spare me a flagon, it will be for medicinal purposes of course and I will not chastise you for selling on the sabbath day".

"Dearest Peter", said the Aleman, "here is our strongest ale I hope this will make well again your visitor", "It will" Peter "It will "

The Aleman passed the flagon over to Peter who took it and walked away in a good stride, the ale man stood hands open waiting for the few pennies in payment, Peter looked back as he took the flagon away, "I thank you for your charity my son", the Aleman rolled his eyes and looked in disbelief at Jervis.

"Can you believe that?" said the Aleman," that I can said Jervis."

Jervis smiled and carried on stoking the fire with wet wood from his wood pile, the smoke and steam bellowed form the forge yard and filled the street, he kept looking toward the top of the village to see if there was any sign of Clara, he imagined here smiling and being happy that Jervis was safe her smiles filled his heart with a joy, this he looked forward to the most.

During that afternoon Jervis wished so hard for the rain to stop, it was making the fire low, he covered it and added more wood, it was hard to find dry wood, the ransacking of his yard the previous night had wetted his wood pile, but he stayed close the fire and kept it alight, it grew in steamy smokey content and soon was deep red and orange in colour, it reacted well to the bellows and finally Jervis felt he was back in control of his world.

He was aware that time was passing on and still no sign of Thomas and Clara and Anna and the four children.

He was hungry so he went to the cottage and put together a plate of food, he spent a little time in the house tidying up and making good the beds ready for the return of his wife and son John.

Peter was busy that evening, he was getting ready for the Sunday service, he had been back and forth up and down the village making sure all his flock would be turning up for the service and telling them why the morning.

In between his to and froing up and down the village, Peter was sitting with Richard Sharnford, Richard had made progress during the day, he had managed to eat some stew and bread, Peter insisted he must eat to build his resolve and strength, Richard complied merely because he was hungry and although the food wasn't the best, it was nourishment, he had slept on and off but was content to sit in the cottage and rest, the arrival of a flagon of ale was very welcome.

CHAPTER 20

Jervis was also feeling the warmth of the ale was worth having, as the rain was constant and the main lane very muddy, he had moved back to the yard to enjoy his plate of food and drink several ales in readiness for the return of his family.

Carltonstone was placed west and east on the old main trackways which crossed the county, sun rises, and sunsets were often spectacular, this evening was promising to be just that, the clouds were breaking up in the distance, the bright red sun flashed its warm light into the village, though the distant turmoil of clouds over Merevale and the hills towards Mancetter and beyond. Promised little respite from the storms of recent weeks.

Jervis glanced up the village again, he was getting more and more irritated that Thomas had not returned but was getting ready to spend the night alone in the yard next to the fire. Jervis poured another drink of Ale, the chapel bell started to ring out, Jervis drank down his ale and with some other villagers made his way down to the chapel. Inside were gathered most of the village, all of them eager for news on the battle of the day before.

Peter stood before them, welcome he said in a quiet voice, yesterday there was a war, during the fighting men were slain, lords were murdered, the King was cut down and killed, the sounds of deep breaths were heard right to the back of the chapel, many in the village were completely unaware of the battle happening only a few miles south of the village.

The room fell silent as the rain hammered on the wooden roof; Peter had to raise his voice to be heard. "We shall prey for those who lost their life in the battle, from commoner, villain to lords and the King."

"It was unfortunate that some of the valorous men were not content with winning the war on the battlefield, they have caused many deaths after the battle, men and women were captured, cut down or killed for no other reason than that of celebration, this sort of celebration is not the drawn from the words of the lord, but an elementary lack of respect for your fellow man."

The congregation sang the few lines of a hymn and psalm was spoken by Peter, he closed the short service by thanking people for coming in such bad rain and asked that they locked doors and kept themselves safe.

The huddle of villages left the small wooden chapel and disappeared into the darkness and rain outside.

Jervis wandered back to the yard and stoked the fire, keeping his eyes out for the cart. After a while and with still no sign he lit a brazier and an oil lamp and placed them outside the yard, so when Thomas came down the lane he would see the light and be guided back, it was still dusk but the rain and heavy clouds made the night seem closer than normal, Jervis settled into his seat in the yard looking across to the cottage and the shutters which needed repairing and after the long summer would need the vines and wild roses cutting back.

In the distance he could hear the odd dog barking, the lane was silent, apart from the sound of the rain splattering on the lean to under which he was sheltering.

He was for the time being content with his thoughts putting together his own list of to do's, as Clara would say.

Then through the silence he thought he heard the rumbling of a cart and what sounded like two horses coming down the lane, he stood up to see in the darkness against a break in the clouds beyond, the outline of a cart and a horse leading, the rain was still coming down, it was difficult to see the outline of the driver or any passengers, but it was getting closer. He stood up but the glare of the rain and the oil lamp made it hard to make out, Jervis stepped though the yard gate and started to walk up the lane, is cap was dripping with the cool water of the night, out of the gloom came a cart, he could see two people on the front, seating, there was one horse leading and the other horses was trailing.

The passengers were silent they had their heads covered with blanket to stave off the worst of the rain Jervis thought.

Jervis called out, "is it you Brother Thomas?" there was no answer, he thought he heard sobbing, but the rain was making such a noise it was hard to make out, the cart stopped some way from Jervis, the horses nodding their heads, Jervis called out again, "is it you brother"?

One of the passengers climbed down from the cart, Jervis held his hand up to his face to shield the light, it could see the outline of the man who walked towards him, as he got closer Jervis called again "Thomas my brother is that you?, Please tell me man", "It is" came the reply.

"Well come on brother you must all be wet through" "Jervis! Stop, but come on let me get to Clara and John, where are they?" Thomas put his hand on Jervis's shoulder "my brother", Jervis interrupted and said, "come on we will all catch a chill come, come, come in the yard all of you I have a fire to warm you!", "Jervis stop listen to me", "Brother what is it?" asked Jervis.

"Brother Jervis, I love you as my brother, I bring you bad news and bad times", why do you bring me bad news Thomas? Jervis was looking hard at Thomas, "where is Anna and Clara?", Jervis looked on the lane to see the other cloaked passenger getting down from the horse and cart and picking up the children from the cart, it was Anna and her three children," where is Clara asked Jervis, his voice getting a serious tone. Thomas took hold of Jervis by each arm and looked directly at him.

"Brother your wife Clara is dead, she passed from this life this morning". Jervis immediately stood back he faltered on his feet for a second, Jervis's eyes were wide, he slowly shook his head, "No, no, no!" and with a dismissive smile he looked further up the lane, and back at Thomas, his lips quivered his eyes welled up, quietly he asked again, "where is she Thomas"?, Jervis looked to his brother for reassurance he was in a dream, a nightmare, "no Thomas, no please, " "am with sorrow brother, Clara is in the back of the cart". Jervis dropped the oil lamp and ran to the back of the cart, he pulled at the back board to get it to drop down, he clawed at it desperately trying to rid his mind of the image he dreaded and did not want to see.

There in the back of the cart was a body, still, lifeless, wrapped in a makeshift shroud, snuggled in alongside it covered in a blanket was his son John sobbing, clinging fast to his mother.

Thomas came to the back of the cart; John has not been able to leave Clara's side he was with her when she passed away.

Jervis fell to his knees in the mud and filth of the lane the rain running down his face, he screamed Nooo! He cried out "Why, why, why? Claaara! He cried a deep tone "Clara my love", as the rain fell into his eyes "oh my lord why?"

Thomas tried to console his brother, but Jervis was having none of this, angrily he pulled away. Thomas didn't know what to do this was something neither brother had suffered. Jervis pulled his cap off his head and sobbed deep sorrowful sobs of grief, John came away from his mothers' body and held his little cold dirty wet hand out for his father, Jervis reached out in the pouring rain fingertips first and took the boy into his arms, the two of them crying, Jervis looking on at the shrouded body being soaked in the rain. Thomas stood side by side his own tears and upset joining in with them.

Anna came to Jervis's side her head covered in a English cap and cape She tenderly held his hand, Anna kissed the boy and Jervis in turn on the cheek, " Jervis I can tell you, she passed quietly and settled with the lord" Anna said, "she had a fever and a sweat I have never seen in any man or woman, it took her first violently and despite trying to keep her it took her away in one night".

Jervis held onto John tightly, "my son my son I am sorry", John held his father in a strong grip, hearing the commotion Peter arrived with a lamp on a pole.

" What is all this about Jervis?", he stood confused at the scene "Jervis, Thomas is everything well"? "No Peter" said Thomas, "we have lost Clara to the French swett".

"My lord oh dear lord god save them" said Peter, he went to the back of the cart, he looked under the blanket at the makeshift shroud, Thomas was with him, " Come bring the cart close to the chapel we will rest her there tonight".

Jervis was sobbing and followed the cart with John in his arms, the rain was cold, miserable, and constant.

Thomas climbed aboard the cart and moved it down the lane to outside the chapel.

Peter and Thomas opened the back of the cart up, Thomas and Peter put the back board down, Jervis handed John to Anna, the other three children watched on in the dim light and pouring rain, Jervis stepped forward and put his hand on the shroud, it was cold and wet to the touch. Jervis, Thomas and Peter lifted Clara's body up, they with slow reverence, slowly walked silently with her in their arms into the chapel where she was lain on a wooden alter quickly prepared by Peter at the front of the chapel.

The three men stood back, for a few moments nothing was said, Peter turned to Jervis, he said "come to me when you are ready", Jervis's eyes were full of tears they rolled down his face, little John arrived and held his father's hand, this made Jervis close his eyes and cry, he sobbed and stepped forward, he with one hand removed the wet should to reveal Clara's face, there before him and in the dim flickering candle light of the chapel, was his wife, she was quiet, still, without any complexion, her hair was coursed across her face, he gathered it and revealed her perfect features, Jervis called her name "Clara, my Clara, I will love you forever"

John called for his mother, in tears Jervis knelt and crossed himself, he held John close by in an embrace.

Peter was standing a little away in the darkness of the shadows, he was whispering prayers, he stopped and quietly went over to stand next to Thomas, He spoke softly to Jervis "come Jervis let Clara rest here we will talk in the morning", "Yes father" said Jervis in a whisper.

Thomas gathered his children and Anna, "come let us go home and settle the children" Thomas said the Anna. The five of them left the chapel.

Peter stepped to the side of Jervis, "my son there is no more that you can do here this night, take John home, put him to bed and rest yourself. I will pray and vigil here until the morning, she will be safe now with me in the house of the lord", Peter hesitated, he drew a deep breath then said "We will make preparations together in the morning".

Jervis was silent, he was holding John, you are ready for a sleep now John said Peter, "be with your father and look after each other tonight. Come to me in the morning", looking down to John he said, "both of you come to me in the morning". Jervis looked down at John, "come John we must leave your mother here to rest" "yes father," said John.

They turned and left the small chapel room, made their way up the village lane, where Thomas was unhitching the two horses and was pushing the cart back into the yard. I am with you brother and with you said Jervis.

Jervis made his way into the cottage, and dried off John, he dressed him in dry clothes and a nightcap, off to bed son, get sleep we will talk together in the morning, Jervis kissed him on the head, and tucked him into the bed.

Jervis returned downstairs and looked to the yard, the glow of the forge fire was inviting, as was the flagon of ale still three quarters full, he put his cap on and made his way across to the yard, the smell of the fire was familiar and comforting.

He settled down poured a drink of ale and sat staring at the flames as they flickered and danced aglow of reds and orange in the great hearth, he covered himself and remained awake for a long time.

He lay there and recalled meeting Clara for the first time she was young and full of life, skilled in her sewing and was always eager to speak to Jervis, her smile and eyes were his wonder.

He remembered how cock proud he was to take her to meet his parents, and how scared he was to meet hers for the first time. He recalled the fear when John was born and not knowing what to do as other women from the village told him to scarper whilst the midwife's attended to Clara.

He drifted off to sleep unaware the John had come across to the yard and settled in besides him, Jervis awoke to find his son huddled up close holding on tightly, Jervis reflected on John face in the fires glow, and how he had some of his mothers' features.

The dawn would be with them in a few hours, again Jervis drifted off the sleep holding his son close.

The following morning, Peter and Thomas came to Jervis with plans to bury Clara that day in the chapel yard, she would be laid to rest under a newly sprouted cherry tree, Jervis and John agreed with this.

Jervis and Thomas set too to dig the grave, there were mourners from the village and Redemoor as the word had been spread quickly around the villages about and tradesmen and messages between them and their customers.

The burial was due to take place in the late afternoon, beforehand Jervis had taken some short time and had walked into the chapel where Clara lay, he touched her cold body, he slowly revealed her face and kissed her gently on the head and bid his darling goodbye.

In this sh'rt life the l'rd giveth and the l'rd taketh hence, valorous people shall liveth 'mongst each oth'r, one shouldst liveth with your own acceptance yond we only passeth this way one's own time.

So, maketh what thee shall of thy time on this earth beest valorous and honest with thy broth'r and neighbour, wend about thy ways in good deed and feareth the l'rd. Maketh well thy life and liveth in peace.

When the time came later that day, John and Jervis led the way into the chapel, Peter had placed Clara in a coffin which was decorated with wildflowers collected by Anna and her children from the fields at the back of the village near to the river.

It was a sombre day and a sad procession, for a change of weather was welcome and on that afternoon the sun shone down. Peter was his usual attentive self, the prayers bought some comfort to Jervis, as they left the chapel yard, Jervis looked across to the rectory and at the window was Richard Sharnford, he nodded his head in the direction of Jervis.

Jervis always remembered how if it wasn't for Richard Sharnford and his protection of Jervis and Thomas, John may have lost both his mother and father in one fateful Saturday morning in 1485.

The events of the last few horrific days were for Jervis, overshadowed by Clara's sudden death from the swett, which came and ravaged most of England and Europe for many years to come,

Jervis and John would never recover from her death, as the years passed Jervis never remarried nor sought comfort. The cherry tree in the chapel yard grew and blossomed a festoon of pink flowers each year, then soon after carpeting the garden below with a confetto of colour, a perfection, reminding them always of Clara.

Jervis bought John up alone and as a good strong and talented blacksmith too, like Jervis's time served it was a long apprenticeship.

Thomas his brother remained as his neighbour, over the next 20 years they saw change in the landscape, they saw the comings and goings of good Kings and lords and the advent of rich wool men and the development of the farming system.

Richard Sharnford eventually recovered from his battle Rout injuries and remained life long and a good friend with Jervis, he became Uncle Richard to John and eventually moved to the village, retiring as King's witness and high Sheriff of the county of Leicestershire.

Thomas had another son by Anna, he bought up both sons to be skilled fletcher's and wood turners working alongside John, they used the yard which stayed as a blacksmiths yard in the village of Carltonstone for almost 300 years, passing through five generations of Blacksmiths and Fletchers, farriers, and wheelwrights.

This st'ry of j'rvis and thomas

smith and fletch'r and the cruel
legacy of the demise of richard
plantagenet endeth h're.

The battle rages as the fallen cry
Victor's cheer and the vanquished die
Smell of fear a circlet his ring of steel.
Stout heart breaks at Bosworth field
The Yorkists men in days of beffore
Fight hand to hand in a stench of blud and gore
All believers trusted in justice are endorsed
They'd followed him there just and because.

Remember well men who to Anne Beame on a hill,
passed this way
Souls of men alive before the misty
dawn on that August day.
Against Henry's odds they would not yield
The lost souls of men who died on
the run from Redemoor feld

The muddi'd, shited and death stench
smelling grounds between dadlyngton
and whytemo'rs in that aft'rnoon wast a
sheet of nak'd bloodi'd bodies and equine
c'rpses, in a yonder timeth aft'r the battle
of hurleyburly those gents w're mutually
and cruelly stripp'd by friendlymen and foe,
local vagabonding gent's and ladies stealing
f'r trinkets and souvenirs, some numb'rs
of these bodies moved as agony and their
kneweth still of their owneth situation
frought them badly, this sight wast one yond
loath'd any god loving, kindly man's eye, but

did remain one f'r hell and its damnation
one couldst not beest did removed.

Some of n'rfolk's men anon did start to fleeth
the battlefield. Seeing this Richard deploy'd
no'rthumb'rland's sizeable contingent to holp
but aft'r having given the 'rd'r the men satteth
th're and didst nothing. At this, l'rd stanley,
seeing the position richard wast in ent'r'd the
battleth. Howev'r that gent didst not ent'r on
richard's side but f'r henry tud'r, his stepson.
Richard hadst taken stanley's son hostage
bef're the battleth to ensureth his loyalty.

That gent may 'r may not has't known yond henry hadst hath met with stanley yond m'rning but t c'rtainly seemeth yond that gent didst not trusteth stanley's loyalty. The O'rd'rs w're cleareth howev'r yond shouldst stanley square f'r henry his son wouldst beest putteth to death. This 'rd'r wast nev'r hath carried ou.

In the hard fighting the Duke of Norfolk was killed (by Sir John Savage, according to the Ballad of Lady Bessy, perhaps while trying to rally his men. After this, the royal army's vanguard started to collapse. According to the Ballad of Lady Bessy, Norfolk was killed near a windmill while fleeing with his troops.

The Dadlington windmill was well over 1,000 yards from the main action, so if Norfolk was killed there it must certainly have been during a rout.

No other source suggests that Norfolk was killed anywhere but in the battle. A livery badge of an eagle was discovered near the mill, so there may well have been some military action here. It seems probable, though, that Norfolk was killed in the battle. Richard, seeing this, feared that Norfolk's death would cause a collapse of morale and thus decided that he should try to bring the battle to an end at a stroke. As Vergil says: 'King Richard understood, where Earl Henry was far off with a small force of soldiers about him, then after drawing nearer he knew it perfectly by evident signs and standards and tokens that it was Henry,

"wherefore all inflamed with ire he struck his horse with spurs and runneth out of the one side without the vanward against him',

"Charging right round Northumberland's right wing and avoiding the marsh. Richard may have hoped that Northumberland would join him.

It must have been a dramatic sight as the King galloped from the side of his army towards Tudor with his troop of horsemen and a 'few footmen'. This elite body of men, formed from the royal household and bodyguard, would have numbered several hundred armed and mounted men. If the King's 'espials' had shown him that Tudor was bearing the undifferenced royal arms to show his pretensions, this might account for a large part of his anger.

While the slaughter of the beaten and fleeing royal army was still taking place, Henry Tudor was busy giving thanks to God for his victory. Then,

"replenish'd with joy incredible", that gent tooketh himself to the nearest hill and commend'd his soldi'rs bef're 'ord'ring the wound'd to beest did look aft'r and the dead corpses to beest did bury"

In the end, however, Richard was killed in battle by Henry whose proclamation said he had been killed at Sandford. The battle ended within a short time, and the royal army fled in a rout of extremes.

Lord Oxford was already beginning to gain the upper hand and it was not long before the van-guard surrendered, and great numbers of them surrendered to Lord Oxford because of the death of Norfolk.

Most of the sources say that many of the royal troops were there reluctantly and were pleased to stop fighting. It is true that many of the levies were reluctant, but what is implied in the sources is that men did not want to fight for Richard and would have fled sooner if they had been able to do so.

Many members of King Richard's army refused to fight for him when he was attained on the grounds that fighting for him was against their "will and mind".

Many also pleaded on the grounds that

"that gent hadst a jointress and eight children who is't w're too young to beest able to supp'rt themselves, and yond t wast contrary to his wife's upbringing to apply f'r alms"

"That gent shouldst loseth his life, lands and goods, yond f'r dread of the same that gent wast most unwillingly at the same field'

Even as the royal army began to flee, the royal army's left wing was likely still resolutely defended by Northumberland and his troops.

Although Northumberland should have charged the French (as he consistently describes Tudor's army), he fled anyway because he had an understanding with Tudor. Northumberland was arrested after the battle, but it is not known if this happened on the battlefield.

According to some recollections and stories, 1,000 of the King's soldiers killed, but only roughly 100 of Tudor's. These estimates may be accurate for the royal army, but they are unacceptably low for Tudor's force.

By mid-morning, the battle might have ended. It lasted more than two hours, according to many stories written in later years, although we don't know when it started.

It's unknown which way the royal forces routed. It appears plausible that they would run north-east, towards Sutton Cheney and away from the enemy, and that some of them would go south.

The discovery of the eagle livery badge at Dadlington mill may indicate that at least some fled to Sutton Cheney. The probable fifteenth-century burials unearthed in and around the churchyard at Dadlington, however, suggest that some people fled south.

In 1511, Henry VIII established a chantry

chapel here to pray for the souls of those killed in the battle, and there is evidence that at least some of the battlefield dead had been transferred to Dadlington churchyard by this time. It's possible that the bones were brought here from where they were originally buried, as was sometimes done when a battlefield chantry was established

While the slaughter of the beaten and fleeing royal army continued, Henry Tudor was busy thanking God for his victory.

Then, "filled with immense joy," he went to the nearest hill and praised his soldiers before ordering that the wounded be cared for and the dead be buried, and that Henry ordered that the dead be given "honourable burials," and that "King Richard himself should be buried with all reverence."

When all present cried 'God save King Henry,' Henry thanked the nobles and commanders with him and knighted some of them, including Rhys ap Thomas, who had brought Welsh troops, and reportedly was responsible for taking Richard's life on the field, with Humphrey Stanley, a distant cousin of Lord Stanley.

Thomas Stanley then crowned him with Richard's crown – that is, the coronet from Richard's helmet. The crown is said to have been discovered in a thorn bush, where it had rolled when Richard was finally killed. It could have been hidden there by a scavenger of bodies for later.

At the end of that day 22nd August 1485. The new King ordered his own pageant to be packed up for moving on, in the evening, his victorious cavalcade left for Leicester, where he entered wearing a new crown.

The procession was accompanied by the late King's naked body, which was treated by fighters and the people of Leicester and surrounding villages with poor respect and lack of reverence for a dead King.

It was said that Richard was dead, tied on the back of a horse with a rope around his neck and his arms and legs hanging down.

He may have been riding his own horse, but it is unfortunate that because Richard lost the battle, his heralds and scribes who probably fled, were unable to record or hold an account of it afterwards. Hence the reliance on accounts today, some written almost 30 years after the battle.

The late King's body was displayed in public in the open for two days in Newark and Leicester to prove that Richard was dead, he was then buried with little royal or civil ceremony. Some later story's say his body was exposed in the Grey Friars' church, in Leicester, but later ballads say it was exposed in Newark on Trent, possibly in the Lancastrian foundation of the Annunciation of Our Lady.

A tomb was later erected in Grey Friars' church by the order of Henry VII some years later, but there is no description of it except that it may have been made of, alabaster and probably had an inscribed effigy of the King on the top.

The tomb, during it is thought the reformation some years later was destroyed, all trace of the original tomb has gone. But we now know he was reburied and his rediscovery in 2012 brings a full circle to the story of the infamous King Richard III and the battle of Bosworth Field, on one misty morning on Saturday August 22nd, 1485, and the grisly end to the Plantagenet ruling of England.

In 2012, archaeologists and researchers discovered a skeleton beneath a car park in Leicester.

The remains were thought to be those of Richard III, the Plantagenet king killed at the Battle of Bosworth in 1485.

I my selfie will hover on
this Anne Beame hill
That ffaire battle ff'r to see.
Sir William, wise and
wealthy, (Stanley)
Was hindmost at the outsetting.
Men said that day that did him see,
He came betime unto our
King [Henry VII]

Then the blew bore the
vanguard had; [Oxford]
He was both warry and wise of witt;

The right hand of them he
took' [the enemy}
The sun and wind of them to get

Sir Perciuall Thriball, the other hight,
& noble Knight, & in his hart was true;
King Richards standard hee kept vpright
vntill both his leggs were hewen him froe;
to the ground he wold neuer lett itt goe,
whilest the breath his brest ws within;
yett men pray ffor the Knights
that euer was soe true to their King.

The Ballad of Bessy was foremost one of the most important references to the battle and it politics, the full story is contained within, and was a favourite recital in many theatres and round houses in the 1500's

That noble knight in the West Countrey,
Tell him that about Michaelmas certaine
In England I do hope to be :
Att Millford haven I will come inn,
With all the power that make may I,
The first towne I will come inn
Shall be the towne of Shrewsbury :
Pray Sir William Stanley, that noble knight,
That night that he will look on me.
Commend me to Sir Gilbert Tallbott, that royall knight,
He much in the North Countrey ;
And Sir John Savage, that man of might,
Pray them all to look on me :
For I trust in Jesus Christ so full of might
In England for to abide and bee.

I will none of thy gold, Sir Prince, said Humphrey
then,
Nor none sure will I have of thy fee ;
Therefore keep thy gold thee within,
For to wage thy company :
If every hair were a man,
With thee, Sir Prince, will I be.

Thus Humphrey Brereton his leave hath tane,
And saileth forth upon the sea ;
Straight to London rideth he then,
There as the Earle and Bessy lay ;
He took them either a letter in hand,
And bad them behold, read and see.
The Earle took leave of Richard the King,
And into the West wind woud he.
He left Bessye in Leicester then,
And bad her lye in privitye ;
For if King Richard knew thee here, anon
In a fire burned must thou be.
Straight to Latham the Earle is gone,
There as the Lord Strange then lee,
He sent the Lord Strange to London
To keep King Richards company.
Sir William Stanley made anone
Ten thousand coats readily,
Which were as redd as any blood,
There on the harts head was set full high,
Which after were tryed both trusty and good
As any coud be in Christantye.
Sir Gilbert Talbot ten thousand doggs
In one hours warning for to be,
And Sir John Savage fifteen white hoods,

Which wou'd fight and never flee,

Edward Stanley had three hundred men,
There were no better in Christentye,
Sir Rees ap Thomas, a knight of Wales certain,
Eight thousand spears brought he.
Sir William Stanley sat in the Holt Castle,
And looked over his head so high ;
Which way standeth the wind, can any tell ?
I pray you, my men, look and see.
The wind it standeth south-east,

So said a knight that stood him by.
This night yonder Prince truely
Into England entereth hee ;
He called a gentleman that stood him nigh,
His name was Rowland of Warburton,
He bad him go to Shrewsbury that night,
And bid yonder Prince come inn ;
But when Rowland came to Shrewsbury,
The port culles it was let downe ;
They called him Henry Tydder in scorn truely,
And said in England he shou'd wear no crowne.
Rowland bethought him of a wyle then,
And tied a writeing to a stone,
And threw the writeing over the wall certain,
And bad the baliffs to look it upon.
They opned the gates on every side,
And met the Prince with procession ;
And wou'd not in Shrewsbury there abide,
But straight he drest him to Stafford towne.

King Richard heard then of his comeing,
He called his Lords of great renowne ;

The Lord Pearcy he came to the King,
And upon his knees he falleth downe :
I have thirty thousand fighting men
For to keep the crown with thee.
The Duke of Northfolk came to the King anone,
And downe he falleth upon his knee ;

The Earle of Surrey, that was his heir,
Were both in one company :
We have either twenty thousand men here
For to keep the crown with thee.
The Lord Latimer, and the Lord Lovell,
And the Earle of Kent he stood him by ;
The Lord Ross, and the Lord Scrope, I you tell
They wer' all in one company ;

The Bishopp of Durham he was not away ;
Sir William Bonner he stood him by :

The good Sir William of Harrington, as I say,
Said he wou'd fight and never fly.

King Richard made a messenger,
And sent him into the West Countrey ;
And bid the Earle of Darby make him bowne,
And bring twenty thousand men unto me,
Or else the Lord Strange his head I will him send,
And doubtless his son shall dye ;
For hitherto his father I took for my friend,
And now he hath deceived me.

Another herald appeared then :
To Sir William Stanley, that doughty knight ;
Bid him bring to me ten thousand men,
Or else to death he shall be dight.

Then answered that doughty knight,
And spake to the herald without letting ;
Say, upon Bosse worth field I mind to fight,
Uppon Monday early in the morning ;
Such a breakfast I him behight,
As never did knight to any King.
The messenger home can him gett,
To tell King Richard this tydeing.
Fast together his hands then cou'd he ding,
And said the Lord Strange shou'd surely dye ;
And putt him into the Tower of London,

For at liberty he shou'd not bee.
Lett us leave Richard and his Lords full of pride,
And talk we more of the Stanley's blood,
That brought Richmond over the sea with wind and
tyde,
From litle Brittain into England over the flood.
Now is Earle Richmond into Stafford come,
And Sir William Stanley to litle Stoone :
The Prince had rather then all the gold in Chris-
tentye
To have Sir William Stanley to look upon.
A messenger was made ready anone,
That night to go to litle Stoon :
Sir William Stanley he rideth to Stafford towne,
With a solemn company ready bowne ;
When the knight to Stafford was comin,
That Earle Richmond might him see,
He took him in his arms then,
And there he kissed him times three :
The welfare of thy body doth comfort me more
Then all the gold in Christantye.

Then answered that royall knight there,
And to the Prince these words spake he ;
Remember man, both night and day,

Who doth now the most for thee ;
In England thou shalt wear a crown, I say,
Or else doubtless I will dye :
A fairer lady then thou shalt have for thy feer,
Was there never in Christanty ;
She is a Countesse, a King's daughter,
And there to both wise and witty.
I must this night to Stone, my soveraigne,
For to comfort my company.

The Prince he took him by the hand,
And said, Farewell, Sir William, fair and free.
Now is word come to Sir William Stanley there,
Earley in the Monday in the morning,
That the Earle of Darby, his brother dear,
Had given battle to Richard the King.
That wou'd I not, said Sir William anone,
For all the gold in Christantye,
That the battle shou'd be done,
Unless that he at the battle shou'd be done ;
Straight to Lichfield cou'd he ride,
In all the hast that might bee ;
And when he came to Lichfield that tyde,
All they, cryed King Henry,
Straight to Bolesworth can they go
In all the hast that might be.
But when he came Bolesworth field unto,
There met a royall company ;
The Earle of Darby thither was come,

And twenty thousand stood him by ;
Sir John Savage, his sisters son,
He was his nephew of his blood so nigh,
He had fifteen hundred fighting men,
That wou'd fight and never flye ;
Sir William Stanley, that royall knight, then
Ten thousand red-coats had he,
They wou'd bicker with their bows there,
They wou'd fight and never flye ;
The Red Ross, and the Blew Boar,
They were both a solemn company.

Sir Rees ap Thomas he was thereby,
With ten thousand spears of mighty tree.
The Earle of Richmond went to the Earle of Darby,
And downe he falleth upon his knee ;
Said, Father Stanley, full of might,
The vaward I pray you give to me,
For I am come to claime my right,

And faine revenged wou'd I bee.

Stand up, he said, my son quickly,
Thou has thy mothers blessing truely,
The vaward, son, I will give to thee,
So that thou wilt be ordered by me :
Sir William Stanley, my brother dear,
In the battle he shall bee ;
Sir John Savage, he hath no peer,
He shall be a wing then to thee ;
Sir Rees ap Thomas shall break the array,

For he will fight and never flee ;
I my selfe will hove on the hill, I say,

The fair battle I will see.
King Richard he hoveth upon the mountaine ;
He was aware of the banner of the bould Stanley,
And said, Fetch hither the Lord Strange certain,
For he shall dye this same day :
To the death, Lord, thee ready make,
For I tell thee certainly
That thou shalt dye for thy uncles sake,
Wild William of Standley.

If I shall dye, said the Lord Strange, then,
As God forbid it shou'd so bee,
Alas, for my Lady that is at home,
It shou'd be long or she see me ;
But we shall meet at dooms day,
When the great doom shall be.
He called for a Gent, in good say
Of Lancashire, both fair and free,
The name of him it was Lathum :
A ring of gould he took from his finger,
And threw it to the Gent, then,
And bad him bring it to Lancashire,
To his Lady that was at home ;
At her table she may sit right,
Or she see her Lord it may be long,
I have no foot to fligh nor fight,
I must be murdered with the King.

If fortune my uncle Sir William Stanley loose the field,
As God forbid it shou'd so bee,
Pray her to take my eldest son and child,
And exile him over behind the sea ;
He may come in another time,

By feild or fleet, by tower or towne,
Wreak so he may his fathers death in fyne,

Upon Richard of England that weareth the crown.

A knight to King Richard then did appeare,
The good Sir William of Harrington : .
Let that Lord have his life, my dear
Sir King, I pray you grant me this boone,
We shall have upon this field anon,
The father, the son, and the uncle all three ;
Then shall you deem, Lord, with your own mouth then,
What shall be the death of them all three.
Then a block was cast upon the ground,
Thereon the Lords head was laid ;
A slave over his head can stand,
And thus that time to him thus said :
In faith there is no other booty tho'
But need that thou must be dead.
Harrington in hart was full woe,
When he saw the Lord must needs be dead :
He said, Our ray breaketh on ev'ry side,
We put our feyld in jeopardie.
He took up the Lord that tyde,
King Richard after did him never see :

Then they blew up the bewgles of brass,
That made many a wife to cry, alas !
And many a wives child father lesse ;
They shott of guns then very fast,
Over their heads they cou'd them throw ;
Arrow's flew them between,
As thick as any hayle or snowe,

As then that time might plaine be seene.
Then Rees ap Thomas with the black raven
Shortly he brake their array ;
Then with thirty thousand fighting men
The Lord Pearcy went his way ;
The Duke of Northfolke wou'd have fledd with a good will
With twentye thousand of his company,
They went up to a wind millne upon a hill
That stood soe fayre and wonderousse hye,
There he met Sir John Savage, a royall knight,
And with him a worthy company.
To the death was he then dight,

And his son prisoner taken was he ;
Then the Lord Alroes began for to flee,
And so did many other moe.
When King Richard that sight did see,
In his heart he was never soe woe ;
I pray you, my merry men, be not away,
For upon this field will I like a man dye,
For I had rather dye this day,
Then with the Standley prisoner for to be.

A knight to King Richard can say there,
Good Sir William of Harrington,
He said, Sir King, it hath no peere
Upon this feild to death to be done,
For there may no man these dints abide ;
Low, your horse is ready at your hand ;
Sett the crown upon my head that tyde,
Give me my battle ax in my hand ;
I make a vow to mild Mary that is so bright,
I will dye the King of merry England.

Besides his head they hewed the crown down right,
That after he was not able to stand ;
They dunge him downe as they were woode,
The beat his bassnet to his head,
Untill the braine came out with bloode ;
They never left him till he was dead.
Then carryed they him to Leicester,
And pulled his head under his feet.

Bessye mett him with a merry cheere,
And with these words she did him greete :
How like you the killing of my brethren dear ?
Welcome, gentle uncle, home !
Great solace it was to see and hear,
When the battle it was all done.
I tell you masters without lett,
When the Red Ross so fair of hew
And young Bessy together mett,
It was great joy I say to you.

Printed in Great Britain
by Amazon